ACCLAIM FOR
BARBARA MICHAELS

"Miss Michaels has a fine sense of atmosphere and story-telling."
—*New York Times*

"A master of the modern Gothic novel."
—*Library Journal*

"A writer so popular that the public library has to keep her books under lock and key."
—*Washington Post*

"Michaels has a fine downright way with the supernatural."
—*San Francisco Chronicle*

"Michaels has a human touch that adds charm to the well-controlled twists and turns."
—*Virginian Pilot/Ledger Star*

"Anyone who craves a remarkable supernatural suspense novel will not want to miss Barbara Michaels. . . . A tremendous reading experience."
—*The Paperback Forum*

"This author never fails to entertain."
—*Cleveland Plain Dealer*

And OTHER WORLDS

"A fascinating foray into mysticism. . . . Michaels . . . turns conventional mystery tradition on its ear. . . . One can only hope that, if this gentleman's club meets again, Michaels will see fit to submit more of their investigations to the public."

—*Omaha World-Herald*

"If you like to feel the little hairs rise up on your arms and wonder about the darkness just on the other side of normal human consciousness, [these] are just the kind of no-frills scary tales for you."

—*Cleveland Plain Dealer*

THE DANCING FLOOR

"Everything a romance reader can ask for."

—*Publishers Weekly*

"Yum, all the ingredients needed to mix one of Michaels's Gothic concoctions."

—*Poisoned Pen*

HOUSES OF STONE

"I wouldn't have missed this for anything. . . . Barbara Michaels has surpassed herself."

—*Phyllis A. Whitney*

"Vivid descriptive writing and convincing dialogue."

—*Publishers Weekly*

"Eerie supernatural events . . . a refreshingly intelligent and unstereotyped heroine."

—*Kirkus Reviews*

VANISH WITH THE ROSE

"I leapt on [this] as if it were chocolate. . . . This book and this writer are addictive."
　　　　　　　　　　—*Alexandra Ripley*

"Involving . . . a cleverly spun mystery."
　　　　　　　　　　—*Booklist*

SHATTERED SILK

"Her most enticing yet . . . will capture any woman's fantasy."
　　　　　　　　　　—*Cleveland Plain Dealer*

"An utterly enchanting book."
　　　　　　　　　　—*Roberta Gellis*

"Super Michaels. . . . Like the antique gowns the heroine collects, *Shattered Silk* glitters!"
　　　　　　　　　　—*Kirkus Reviews*

HERE I STAY

"An absolutely first-rate job of summoning up the spooky . . . takes on the added dimension besides that of a very good ghost story."
　　　　　　　　　　—*Publishers Weekly*

"Scary, interesting. A winner."
　　　　　　　　　　—*Pittsburgh Press*

SMOKE AND MIRRORS

"Michaels delivers another sure-fire winner!"
　　　　　　　　　　—*Publishers Weekly*

"The perfect curl-up-at-homer for a frosty . . . eve."
　　　　　　　　　　—*New Woman*

HarperChoice

OTHER WORLDS

BARBARA MICHAELS

HarperPaperbacks
A Division of HarperCollinsPublishers

HarperPaperbacks
A Division of HarperCollins*Publishers*
10 East 53rd Street, New York, NY 10022-5299

This is a work of fiction. The characters, incidents, and
dialogues are products of the author's imagination and are not to
be construed as real. Any resemblance to actual events or
persons, living or dead, is entirely coincidental.

The second of the two cases published herein originally
appeared in a slightly different form as "Strange Affair at Stratford" in *Tales of the Uncanny* published by The Reader's Digest
Association, Inc. Reprinted by permission.

ISBN 0-06-109749-7

HarperCollins®, 📖®, HarperPaperbacks™, and HarperChoice™
are trademarks of HarperCollins Publishers Inc.

Cover design by Gene Mydlowski

Cover type © 1999 by Saska Art & Design

Cover illustration © 1998 by Donna Diamond

A hardcover edition of this book was published in 1999
by HarperCollins*Publishers*.

First HarperPaperbacks printing: February 2000

Printed in the United States of America

Visit HarperPaperbacks on the World Wide Web at
http://www.harpercollins.com

❖ 10 9 8 7 6 5 4 3 2 1

To Joan Hess
With profound affection and admiration

OTHER WORLDS

The First Evening

ONE

THE SCENE is the smoking room of an exclusive men's club, familiar through film and fiction even to those who have been denied admittance to such precincts because of deficiencies of sex or social status. The lamplight glows on the rich rubbed leather of deep, high-backed chairs. Grave, deferential servants glide to and fro, their footsteps muffled by the thick carpet. The tall windows are draped in plum-red plush, shutting out the night air and the sounds of traffic on the street without—the traffic, perhaps, of hansom cabs and horse-drawn carriages. For this is no real establishment; it exists outside time and space, in the realm of the imagination—one of the worlds that might have been.

A small group of men enters the room. They have the sleek, satisfied look of gentlemen who have dined well, and who are looking forward to brandy and a fine Havana and another pleasure equally as great—conversation with their peers on a subject deeply engrossing to all of them.

One man leads the way, striding impatiently. His high forehead is wrinkled, his eyes narrowed. Mr. Frank Podmore calls himself "skeptic-in-chief" of the Society for Psychical Research. The spiritualist tricksters he has exposed, and many of his own colleagues in the SPR, consider him unreasonable and unfair. Those colleagues would recognize the expression on his face this evening. Podmore is on the trail again, ready to pour the ice-water of his doubt on another questionable case.

Behind him comes a man whose voice still retains the accents of his native Vienna—Nandor Fodor, formerly director of the International Institute for Psychical Research, who resigned in disgust when his colleagues objected to his "filthy-minded" explanations of certain cases. A practicing psychiatrist for many years, he has investigated almost as many purported "ghosts" as has Podmore.

The third member of the group is stocky and clean-shaven, with keen blue-gray eyes. Born Erik Weisz, son of a Hungarian rabbi, he is better known as Harry Houdini. Many of the spiritualists he ridiculed claimed that he himself must have had psychic powers in order to accomplish his amazing feats.

One of his old antagonists, a burly man with a

bristling mustache and soft blue eyes, walks with him. Conan Doyle and Houdini broke off their friendship when Houdini attacked Doyle's faith in the survival of the dead. It would be pleasant to believe that in some other time and place these two good men have at last made up their quarrel.

A fifth person follows modestly behind the others. From his hesitant manner and the formal way in which the others address him, one might deduce that he is a guest, rather than a regular member of the group. He is taller and heavier than the others; his evening suit is a trifle old-fashioned and more than a trifle too small. He has very large feet.

They settle into their chairs. Topaz liquid swirls in the bell-shaped glasses and a fragrant fog of smoke surrounds them.

"Well, gentlemen," says Podmore, "are we ready to begin?" Typically, he does not wait for a reply, but continues, "Tonight's case—"

Doyle raises a big hand. "Always impatient, Podmore. Don't you think we owe our guest a word of explanation first? He knows our purpose, but cannot be familiar with our methods."

"Oh—certainly." Podmore turns to the stranger. "I beg your pardon, sir. All of us have investigated many cases of presumed supernatural activity, some as agents of the SPR and some, like Houdini, in a private capacity. During our evenings together we enjoy a busman's holiday, applying our combined expertise to the investigation of famous cases that have never been satisfactorily explained. Sometimes we agree on a solution; more often we agree to disagree."

"More often?" Fodor repeats, smiling. "I cannot remember an occasion when the verdict was unanimous, and I know none of you are going to agree with my solution to this case. The Bell Witch, is it not?"

"Correct," says Podmore. "And, as is fitting, we have selected our American member to describe this American ghost. No more interruptions, gentlemen, if you please; pray, silence for Mr. Harry Houdini."

Houdini has his notes ready. He gives the others a rueful smile. "This is worse than escaping from a sealed coffin, gentlemen. Book research isn't my style, and this is the first case I've investigated where all the suspects have been dead for over a century. But as Podmore would say, that just makes it more challenging. And what a tale it is! Dr. Fodor here has called it the greatest American ghost story. I would go further; I would call it the greatest of all ghost stories. There is nothing to equal it on either side of the Atlantic.

"Over the years the true facts have become so encrusted with layers of exaggeration, misinterpretation, false memories and plain out-and-out lies that the result sounds like one of Sir Arthur's wilder fictions. Our greatest difficulty will be to figure out what really happened. I won't presume to do that; I will just give you the story as I have worked it out and let you decide what is important and what isn't. Ready? Then here we go."

TWO

B ETSY BELL was twelve years old when the witch
came.

It sounds like the beginning of one of the fairy tales
beloved by juvenile readers, a tale in the great tradition
of the Brothers Grimm. Even the name of the heroine
conjures up the image of a smiling, dimpled child with
bows on her pigtails, skipping merrily through the
woods with a basket on her arm!

But Betsy's witch was no Hallowe'en hobgoblin
with a pointed hat and a broomstick, and by the time it
finally left the Bell household, Betsy was a young
woman of seventeen who had seen her lover driven
away and her father tormented into his grave. Betsy is
certainly the heroine of our tale—a tale of horror so fan-

tastic no writer of fiction would dare invent it. But she is not the chief protagonist. That distinction belongs to another character.

In the early part of the nineteenth century, Robertson County, Tennessee, was being settled by easterners looking for new land. It was not wild frontier country; the only Indians in the region were those whose dry bones lay buried in the grassy mounds scattered about the countryside. Most of the settlers were well-to-do farmers and slaveowners. The little community was civilized enough to possess a school, presided over by a handsome young master, and several churches. The oldest of these houses of worship, the Red River Baptist Church, had been founded in 1791. Some of the settlers belonged to this church, some to that of the Methodists, but petty sectarian differences did not divide them; an admirable spirit of Christian tolerance prevailed.

The country these men and women discovered was a lovely land of rolling hills and stately forests, of fertile meadows and rippling streams—an abundant land, giving freely of its riches. Game abounded in the woods, the virgin soil provided grain and vegetables, maple syrup flowed from the trees, and fish fairly leaped out of the river to snatch the angler's hook.

Into this earthly paradise, in the year 1804, came Mr. John Bell and his family. John and his wife, Lucy, were from North Carolina. Mrs. Bell, a good Christian woman, had obeyed the Biblical injunction to be fruitful and multiply. By 1804 she had given birth to six children.

The size of their growing family and the urgent invitations of friends who had already settled in the west convinced Mr. Bell to emigrate. He sold his farm in North Carolina for such a good price that he was able to buy a thousand acres of land in Tennessee, along the Red River.

There was a house on the property, built of logs and covered with clapboard. It was one of the finest homes in the county, with six large rooms and a parlor, called a "reception room" in those days. An "ell," or wing, contained several more rooms and a passageway. A wide porch stretched across the front of the house, looking out over a vista of green lawns shaded by fine old pear trees. It must have been a pleasant place to sit on spring afternoons, when the trees were masses of snowy blooms, and the Bells welcomed visitors hospitably. John Bell made his own whiskey of pure spring water, and I assure those of you who have not tried it that there is no finer beverage. Drunkenness was a sin, of course, but there was nothing wrong with an occasional nip, "to sharpen one's ideas."

With the help of his neighbors the industrious Mr. Bell cleared more land and built barns and slave quarters. Soon after they arrived Mrs. Bell had another child—a daughter, who was named Elizabeth. Two more children followed in due course. By the fateful spring of 1817 only one of the Bells' offspring slept in the family cemetery on the gravelly ridge behind the house, his grave shaded by cedar and walnut trees. One out of nine is an amazing survival record for that time; perhaps the healthy life and the clean country air had something to do with it. Cynics might claim that the absence of medical attention also helped, but this would not be entirely accurate. The community possessed several doctors, one of whom, Dr. George Hopson, attended the Bells in cases of severe illness. We will meet Dr. Hopson in due course, when he was confronted with a case that would try the skill of any physician.

Though we have been formally introduced to Mr. and Mrs. Bell, we do not know them well. In attempting to sketch their portraits we suffer from the commendable yet frustrating refusal of survivors to speak ill of the dead. No candid comments have come down to us, no faded photographs survive; we can only sketch verbal portraits, vague and incomplete. Yet by piecing together a fact here and a casual comment there, we can derive some notion of what the actors in this eerie drama were like.

Simple arithmetic tells us that if John Bell was born in 1750 (which he was), he was sixty-seven years of age in 1817, when the trouble began. Despite his age, he was as hale and hearty as many a man twenty years his junior. (Bear in mind, my friends, that his last child had been born when he was sixty-two.) Unlike the aristocratic planters of the southeastern states, the Washingtons and Jeffersons and Lees, Mr. Bell was no gentleman of leisure, but a farmer who worked with his own hands. His children praised him as God-fearing and industrious, sober and devout. We need not take these epitaphs too literally, but we must admit we know nothing to his discredit. If his children fail to mention laughing and romping with their father, they are equally silent about harsh punishments. He was certainly a devout Christian; his was one of the homes in which weekly prayer meetings were held. Yet it would be a mistake to picture this patriarch as a dour Puritan. He had at least one amiable human quality—he was not stingy with his whiskey.

Lucy Bell, affectionately known to her friends as "Luce," was approximately fifteen years younger than her husband. Her children had not acquired the now-fashionable habit of blaming all their troubles on their parents; they spoke of Lucy with the highest praise. She was, simply, the best woman living. Many years later Richard Williams Bell wrote of his mother that she was "greatly devoted to the moral training of her children, keeping a restless watch over every one, making sacrifices for their pleasure and well-being." A curious word to choose—restless. But perhaps Richard only meant untiring.

We may be sure her duties were unceasing and tiring. Modern ladies who complain of their hard lives would take to their beds after a few days of Lucy Bell's routine. The settlers imported few luxuries. Almost everything they required was produced on their farms—the food they ate, the clothing that covered their bodies, the furniture and farm equipment they used. Cobblers and carpenters and coopers, seamstresses and spinners and cooks were, most of them, slaves, but these workers required constant supervision. Besides, the religion followed by the Bells and their neighbors taught that idleness was a sin. Even their social pleasures, such as barn raisings and corn huskings, involved hard labor—and the women worked as hard as the men, cooking vast quantities of food for the workers and occupying their spare time with sewing and mending. Lucy Bell's hands were never idle except when they were folded in prayer.

At the time of the witch's persecution only five of the Bell children were living at home. The youngest was little Joel, just four years old. Richard was six, golden-haired Betsy, the only remaining daughter, was twelve "going on thirteen." Drewry was sixteen, and John Junior a grown man of twenty-two.

A dashing young fellow, six feet two inches tall and powerfully built, John Junior had qualities—imagination, daring, restlessness—the others lacked. Finding himself one day in the nearby town of Springfield, he had seen a recruiting poster and enlisted in the army. The United States was at war—one of our minor wars, a little spat with England over the question of impressing sailors from American ships. You British did well in the east, burning the half-built capital and sending Dolley Madison scampering for safety with Washington's portrait under her arm. But Britain lost that war, thanks in part to the military skill of a fiery Tennessean,

Andrew Jackson, who was to become the nation's seventh president.

John Bell Junior served under Andy Jackson in the campaign that ended in the Battle of New Orleans, where a rabble of backwoods hunters thumped the British regulars. John was among these riflemen; he could "bark" a squirrel from a tall tree, shooting its perch out from under it without touching it. No doubt he celebrated the victory in the genial taverns of New Orleans. It was a charming city even then; small wonder that after being mustered out John Junior refused to stay down on the farm, but found excuses to return to the bright lights and the charming Creole ladies.

Being a discreet and ingenious young man, he discovered a practical excuse for traveling. Before the advent of the steamboat, goods were transported from the interior of the country by means of flatboats—an exceedingly economical method of transportation, requiring only strong muscles and a few crudely hewn planks. The boats were built on the banks of the river during the late summer and fall and cabled to trees until the spring thaw caused the water to rise high enough to float them. From the Red River, which flowed by the Bells' farm, to the Cumberland and into the Ohio, the swift current led finally onto the broad bosom of the Father of Waters, all the way south to New Orleans. Hams and whiskey, tobacco and corn, and other native products brought a handsome profit in the markets of the city. His brother Drewry was one of John's partners in this enterprise, and he had no trouble finding other young men anxious to share in the profit and the fun. Once the boats were unloaded in New Orleans they were abandoned or sold for scrap lumber, and the daring boatmen set out for home, on horseback or shank's mare. The uncertainties of such forms of travel gave them plenty of time to amuse themselves in the city and on the return trip—with no embarrassing questions asked when they arrived home.

John must have started this business almost as soon as he was discharged from the army. His last trip took place in the spring of 1818. An invoice dated April of that year indicated that fifty hogsheads of tobacco brought eighteen hundred dollars in cash, two hundred dollars' worth of sugar and coffee, plus two hundred pair of boots.

Why, we might ask, did John abandon this lucrative trade? For one thing, steamboats were rapidly replacing the slower, clumsier rafts. There may have been another reason. When John returned to Tennessee in May 1818, he found a desperate situation at home.

THREE

THE TROUBLE had actually begun a year earlier, in the spring of 1817. The first of the family to see something strange was John Bell Senior, but he attached no significance to the incident at the time, only thought it mildly curious. He had left the house after breakfast in order to give his instructions to the overseers. As he strode briskly toward the north end of the farm, where the men were to work that day, he carried his rifle over his shoulder in the hope of getting a shot at a rabbit or some other tasty addition to the menu. Instead of a rabbit he saw, between two rows of corn, a peculiar-looking animal that resembled a large dog.

The creature must have been very peculiar indeed, for John Bell fired at it. He would not have done this if he had thought it was a domestic animal belonging to one of his neighbors. The creature promptly vanished. Mr. Bell assumed he had missed and that the animal had taken to its heels. He thought no more about the matter—then.

A few days later Betsy and Drewry reported seeing strange creatures about the place. Betsy also saw a woman strolling in the orchard. When she spoke to it, the apparition disappeared.

No doubt Mr. Bell dismissed these tales as the products of youthful imagination. He had no reason then to connect them with another bewildering set of phenomena that began about this time—knocks and raps on the doors, and scratching sounds on the outer walls of the house. These could also be rationally explained. Wild animals may approach quite close to a dwelling to forage for scraps. Raccoons have been known to gnaw at wooden door frames; rats and mice invade even a well-run house. Gradually, however, the knocking at the door became so distinct as to suggest that someone was demanding entry. But when the door was flung open, no one was there.

All through that summer and into the following fall and winter the unseen trickster continued its odd pranks. Mr. Bell decided neighborhood children must be responsible. The disturbances were mild and caused the Bells only minor inconvenience. The younger members of the family were not even aware of them at first, since they usually occurred after dark when Betsy and Joel and Richard had gone to bed.

Then, almost a year after they had begun, the sounds found a way into the house. Richard Bell never forgot that night.

The day was Sunday, sometime in the month of May 1818. The family had gone to bed. The boys shared a single bedroom, John and Drewry occupying one of the big double beds and Joel and Richard the other. Betsy's room was across the hall. The parents slept on the ground floor, in a chamber directly under Betsy's.

The candles had been put out and the boys were settling down to sleep when Richard heard a sound like a rat gnawing on the bedpost, not far from his head. The others heard it, too. The older boys jumped up and lit a candle, ready to kill the offensive intruder, but as soon as they got out of bed the sounds stopped. Examination of the post, and the rest of the bedstead, showed no marks of gnawing.

The boys went back to bed. As soon as they lay down, the noises resumed, only to cease when they arose. This went on for hours, till long after midnight. The exasperated boys searched the room again and again, finding no sign of a rodent or even a hole by which one might have entered.

This procedure continued night after night, week after week. Betsy's room was also affected; the sounds moved to her chamber while the boys were searching theirs. No one could sleep, particularly after the sounds increased in intensity. Now they resembled the scratching of a dog instead of a smaller animal such as a rat.

The Bells extended their search to other rooms of the house, stripping the beds and moving the furniture, but found no evidence of an animal's presence, or any means by which it could have found its way in.

Before long the invisible creature began to vary its performance. One new sound was a bizarre gulping and smacking. The bedcovers started to slip off the beds. Noises like heavy rocks falling and massive chains being dragged across the floor kept the bewildered Bells up until one or two in the morning.

It is said that familiarity breeds contempt. It also breeds indifference. The family got used to the mysterious noises. They were only noises, after all, and had not harmed anyone except by depriving them of sleep. The Bells took to snatching naps during the daytime. As if annoyed at being ignored, the intruder moved to direct action. It is no wonder that many years later Richard retained the most vivid memories of this first physical attack.

"I had just fallen into a sweet doze when I felt my hair beginning to twist—then a sudden jerk, which raised me. It felt like the top of my head had been taken off."

Richard let out a yell. His little brother Joel began to scream. An invisible hand was tugging at his hair, too. Then came a shriek from Betsy, across the hall. She continued to scream until her parents rushed upstairs to see what was the matter.

They found Betsy sitting up in bed, shaking from

head to foot. Her luxuriant golden hair hung tangled and twisted around her shoulders. The child was so upset that her parents had to take her to their room for the remainder of the night.

From then on, the disturbances were impossible to ignore. The children were constantly tormented, the coverings ripped from their beds, their hair pulled ruthlessly. At times the house fairly shook with raps and rumblings. John Bell clung stoutly to rational explanations. Remembering a minor earthquake that had struck the area a few years earlier, he wondered if a similar natural cause might not be responsible for the reverberations that rattled the house. But an earthquake could not tug at a child's hair, or cause the strange illness that began to affect Mr. Bell. It felt like a stick laid crosswise in his mouth, with the ends jabbing into his cheeks, and caused his tongue and jaws to swell so badly that while the effect lasted he could scarcely eat or speak.

One source of Mr. Bell's bewilderment was that he had no convenient label for what was happening. Witchcraft? Superstition dies hard; the family slaves whispered of haunts and witches around their cabin fires, and the children had probably listened to their tales in delighted horror. Betsy's reports of apparitions and strange animals were undoubtedly derived from such sources. As everyone knew, witches could transform themselves into cats, dogs, and hares. They also nurtured familiars, demons in animal shape who assisted them in their evil tricks. But Mr. and Mrs. Bell were not superstitious. Not then or ever did Mr. Bell yield to the temptation to ascribe his sufferings to a malevolent witch. Disembodied spirits, then? The year was 1818; it would be another twenty years before the merry little Fox sisters of Hydesville, New York, learned how to crack their knee joints and produce the rappings that heralded the birth of modern spiritualism. The Bells were unacquainted with seances and spirit guides. They had never heard the word *poltergeist*.

Being more experienced, we know that this German term means "noisy spirit," and we are familiar with hundreds of such cases, from the earliest times to the present day. If the Society for Psychical Research had been in existence in 1818, and if John Bell had consulted its experts, the verdict would have been unanimous, for mysterious raps and scratching sounds, unexplained movements of objects such as bedclothes, and even slaps and pinches are typical of the tricks in the poltergeist's repertoire.

Let us then clarify our terminology. The Bell Witch was no witch. We may as well give it the name the Bells used when referring to it—a Spirit—and we will grant it a capital letter, like a given name, for the entity had its own distinct personality—one more vivid in some ways than the living persons it persecuted. Like a human child, it grew and developed with the passage of time.

Of course the word *poltergeist* is not an explanation, it is only a description, and John Bell would not have been comforted by the knowledge that the strange force could be classified. And indeed, in this case the experts would have been in for a shock, for after a relatively tame beginning the Bell Spirit would prove to be unique in the annals of poltergeistery.

FOUR

For a long time the Bells kept silent about
their "trouble," as they called it. It is hard to
believe that none of the neighbors knew what was
going on; surely the slaves must have whispered among
themselves, or the younger children complained to
playmates. Little Joel was only five; he could hardly be
expected to understand why he shouldn't tell his
friends about the horrid thing that tugged at his curls
and jerked the covers off his bed. Be that as it may, no
one outside the family was officially informed about
what was happening until matters got so bad that Mr.
Bell decided to confide in his best friend.

James Johnson was the Bells' nearest neighbor, as
devout a Methodist as they were Baptists. The denomi-

national differences did not prevent the families from being close. Mr. Johnson took turns with the Bells in holding weekly prayer meetings that members of both churches attended. Johnson's two sons, John and Calvin, were also on excellent terms with the Bells, and his adopted daughter, Theny, was Betsy's chum.

We can readily imagine Mr. Johnson's consternation and concern on hearing his friend's amazing story. He immediately agreed to come and spend the night, to observe the phenomena at first hand and see what, if anything, could be done.

Mr. and Mrs. Johnson duly arrived and were entertained by the Bells with their usual hospitality. John and Lucy must have found it an enormous relief to talk about their experiences. Evening drew on, and as the shadows gathered, the Bells and their visitors adjourned to the reception room for prayers. Mr. Johnson was a noted lay preacher, admired for his fluent tongue. On this occasion he outdid himself, leading the group in a hymn and praying for the deliverance of his friends from their affliction. When it was time to retire the Johnsons were given the room next to Betsy's.

No sooner had the visitors climbed into bed than the fun began—scratching, knocking, growls, and the uncanny gulping and smacking. Mr. Johnson got out of bed and struck a light. As usual, this put an end to the activity in his room, but the sounds only moved elsewhere. Accompanied by the Bells, Johnson followed the sounds from room to room, increasingly awed and amazed. He was particularly struck by one set of noises—the smacking as of invisible lips and the impression of air being sucked between the teeth. Was it possible, he wondered, that the unseen entity had a mouth capable of speech?

"In the name of the Lord," he cried. "Who are you? What do you want? Why are you here?"

The sounds stopped. The Bells stared at one another. It had not occurred to them that their tormentor might be able to hear and understand. Alas, though Mr. Johnson's questions received a response, it was not the one he had hoped for. The raps and rattles broke out again, louder than before. Betsy shrieked and clutched at her head as something tugged viciously at her golden locks, bringing them tumbling down her back.

A badly shaken Mr. Johnson threw up his hands. "It is beyond my comprehension," he confessed. "It is evidently preternatural or supernatural, but clearly of an intelligent character. Did it not cease action when spoken to? I advise you, my poor friend, to invite other friends into the investigation and try all means to detect the mystery."

Mr. Bell took Johnson's advice. The Bell Spirit ceased to be a private "family trouble" and turned into a neighborhood circus or sideshow. Scarcely an evening passed without a group of spectators sitting around the fire in the reception room hoping for a demonstration of mysterious powers.

Not all the visitors were moved by idle curiosity. Mr.

and Mrs. Johnson and their sons were constant in their attentions, and the ministers of the local churches lent spiritual comfort. The Bells' pastor was Reverend Fort, of the Drakees Pond Baptist Church. The Methodist ministers, James and Thomas Gunn, were closely connected with the family by ties of kinship as well as affection. Jesse Bell, John and Lucy's oldest son, had married Martha Gunn, the daughter of Reverend Thomas, and in due course three more of the Gunn girls would marry into the Bell family.

In the presence of these pious and intelligent gentlemen the demonstrations not only continued but increased. Strange lights were seen around the fields and farmyard; sticks and pieces of wood pelted the boys when they came in from work in the evening. Mr. Johnson insisted that the manifestations were produced by a guiding intelligence, and he continued to question it: "How many fingers am I holding up?" "How many people are present?" Eventually answers came, by means of raps or scratches. It never occurred to this innocent gentleman, untrained in the techniques of the spiritualist seance, to demand that the Spirit reply to more complex enquiries by spelling out its responses alphabetically. He exhorted the Spirit to speak—and it did.

FIVE

PICTURE THE SCENE, gentlemen, in all its antique charm: the women in their prim print dresses and aprons, the sober, bearded faces of the men, eerily shadowed by the glow of the fire. A few candles and lamps added to the illumination, but by modern standards the room was dark and the furnishings were of Spartan simplicity—straight wooden chairs, braided rugs made by Mrs. Bell and her servants, a cupboard holding the glasses in which Mr. Bell was accustomed to serve his excellent whiskey; on the wall, perhaps, a sampler embroidered by Betsy, with pious Biblical verses worked in colored wools. Picture, as well, the looks of surprise and horror and morbid fascination as that first faint whispering reply is heard.

At first the Spirit had trouble speaking, as if it were experimenting with a type of apparatus unfamiliar to it, or in poor repair. The initial sounds were faint and broken, interspersed with whistling breaths; but as the audience continued to question it the voice gained strength and distinctness. Its first coherent utterance seems to have been a repetition of Mr. Johnson's prayer and hymn delivered on the night he first encountered the Spirit. The voice sounded exactly like his.

The response to this performance must have gratified the Spirit. On succeeding occasions it demonstrated an astonishing knowledge of Scripture and a talent for debate. Its own voice was exceedingly sweet; it enjoyed singing and knew every hymn in the book.

Intrigued as they were by this insane parlor game, some of the visitors never lost sight of their main interest—to discover what the entity was and why it had come. If they could learn its origin and purpose, they might find out how to get rid of it. After hours of interrogation the voice finally answered the oft-repeated question.

"I am a spirit who was once very happy, but have been disturbed and made unhappy."

A thrill ran through the assembled group when this faltering explanation was heard. Excited questions followed. Why was it unhappy? What had happened to disturb it?

Solemnly the mysterious voice explained that it was the spirit of a person who had been buried in the nearby woods. "My grave has been disturbed, my bones disinterred and scattered. One of my teeth was lost under this house and I am here looking for that tooth."

Ridiculous, of course! But we can hardly blame the beleaguered Bells for grasping at any straw. One of the family recalled a half-forgotten event of three or four years earlier, when some of the farmhands, clearing land, found a group of graves. Old Indian cemeteries were common in the region. Mr. Bell ordered his men to work carefully around it without disturbing the dead.

However, his son Drewry mentioned the discovery to a friend and this young man, Hall by name, suggested that they dig up the graves in order to look for relics.

Hoping for tomahawks and arrowheads, they were disappointed to find only scattered bones. Idly, young Hall picked up a jawbone and carried it back to the house. No doubt he and Drew handled the fragment unceremoniously, joking and laughing with the frivolity of youth. Hall finally threw it against the wall. One of the teeth was jarred loose and dropped into a crack in the floor. Mr. Bell happened to pass by just then and was annoyed at the boys' irreverence. After scolding them, he ordered one of the slaves to return the jawbone and fill in the grave.

Undoubtedly the whole family knew about this incident, but they had forgotten it until the Spirit jogged their memories. Mr. Bell thought the matter worth investigating, but though the floor was taken up and the dirt beneath sifted, no tooth was found. After the work was finished, the Spirit laughed. "It was just a joke to fool old Jack Bell," it remarked.

This performance ought to have made the Bells wary of any similar explanation offered by their uncanny guest, but the Spirit's next invention was accepted even more eagerly, perhaps because it was sweetened with an appeal to greed.

"I am the spirit of an early immigrant. I brought a large sum of money and buried it for safekeeping until it was needed. In the meantime I died without divulging the secret and I have returned in the spirit for the purpose of making known the hiding place. I want Betsy Bell to have the money."

Betsy probably felt she deserved it. The Spirit had taken to slapping her as well as pulling her hair.

After waving this golden bait before the audience, the Spirit played coy. It insisted on a number of arbitrary conditions before it consented to tell where the treasure was buried. Drew Bell and his brother-in-law Bennett Porter must do the actual digging. Mr. Johnson, whom it referred to familiarly as "Old Sugar Mouth," must go with them to make sure the work was properly carried out and to ensure that every penny of the treasure would go to Betsy.

There was laughter and incredulity at this remarkable offer, but in the end the persons mentioned decided to have a go at it. Don't look superior, gentlemen; wouldn't you have done the same? The Spirit's directions were detailed: the money was buried under a large flat rock on the southwest corner of the farm, near the river. It obviously knew every inch of the property.

So the party got up at the crack of dawn—obeying another of the Spirit's demands—and set out, shovels and pickaxes in hand. The rock was enormous and so deeply sunk in the earth that it took the sweating boys hours to raise it. There was nothing underneath but dirt.

After some angry discussion, the party decided not to give up yet. Mr. Johnson had helped with the raising of the stone. Now he sat down to rest and supervise while Drew and Bennett dug. By the time the light began to fail they had excavated a hole six feet square and almost as deep without finding anything.

Disheveled, dirty and disgusted, the duped party returned to the house. When they were relaxing in the reception room after supper the voice of the Spirit was heard, cackling with laughter over the trick it had played on them.

"Drew can handle a sight of dirt," it chortled. "His hands were made for that, and are better than a shovel. No gold can slip through his fingers. And Old Sugar Mouth looked on, praying and encouraging the boys. Oh, how it made them sweat!"

Its mirth was contagious. The whole family— except, perhaps, the exhausted Drew—burst into peals of laughter.

The visitors continued to ask questions and the Spirit continued to tease them. It informed Calvin Johnson it was the ghost of a child buried in North Carolina; Calvin's brother John was told that it was the witch of his stepmother. Its next invention was not so harmless.

"I am the witch of old Kate Batts, and I have come to torment Jack Bell until he dies."

In another time and place this malicious lie might have had serious consequences. For in that quiet rural community there was no more suitable candidate for the position of witch than Mrs. Kate Batts.

We all know, gentlemen, that it is not advisable to allow the ladies to go into trade or follow masculine professions. There is a danger they may find out they are as competent as we! The illness of her husband had forced Mrs. Batts to play a man's role, and she had displayed a remarkable aptitude for business. The family was well-to-do, with a good farm and many slaves. In addition to running the farm Kate had developed a nice trade in woolen goods, keeping her slave women busy spinning and weaving and sewing. This gave her an excuse to call on her neighbors, selling the finished product and buying raw wool. She was an immensely stout woman, and when she set out on her weekly circuit at the head of her troop of servants, she gave the neighborhood quite a show. A servant girl led the way, with Kate's old gray horse. Kate walked behind, dressed in her finest clothes. She had never been seen to ride the horse.

If Kate Batts had been poor and meek, her eccentricities might have gotten her into trouble. Being wealthy, and the possessor of a particularly vicious tongue, she enjoyed the unwilling respect of her acquaintances. They got their revenge on her by laughing at her behind her back and by repeating stories of her odd behavior—like the time she sat down on a repentant sinner at a revival meeting, and pressed the poor man half to death before he could gasp out a confession of sin and a plea for salvation.

When word reached Mrs. Batts that the Bell Spirit had claimed to belong to her, there was music in the breeze, as a contemporary witness put it. Her eyes flashed and her tongue flapped at both ends, spitting out curses mixed with the malapropisms for which she was famous. She could not have invented a better defense; the grim accusation became just another funny story about crazy Kate Batts.

Still, there were a few superstitious people who believed it, especially when they remembered that John Bell had once gotten the better of Kate in a business transaction, and that she had told him what she thought of him in no uncertain terms. These people whispered of Kate's mysterious powers—which no one had happened to notice before the Spirit spoke. So the strange entity that haunted the Bells became known as a witch, and from then on it readily answered when visitors addressed it as "Kate."

It was a harmless conclusion to an affair that might have ended with the gibbet or the noose or mob violence, and part of the credit must go to John Bell, who consistently and vehemently scoffed at the accusation. Yes, Mrs. Batts had called him rude names and promised to get even with him; she had done the same to other people who had proved sharper in trade. No doubt she was peculiar, but she was a good, pious woman at heart, and the idea of witchcraft was absurd.

As if annoyed at John Bell's contradiction of its claim, the Spirit proceeded to try his patience to the limit. It introduced four new characters—an entire Witch family. Their names were Blackdog, Mathematics, Cypocryphy and Jerusalem, and the voice that had hitherto been sweet and soft changed to suit these personalities. Blackdog, the head of the family, spoke in a harsh but distinctly feminine voice. Jerusalem's tones were those of a young boy. Mathematics and Cypocryphy had different voices, but both were female. However, their language was quite unbecoming to the gentle sex. The vilest blasphemies and threats shocked the listeners. They sounded, said Richard succinctly, "like a lot of drunken men fighting."

Vicious threats against John Bell constituted part of the performance, and Mr. Bell seriously considered abandoning his home and moving away. Useless, jeered the "witch family"; they would follow Old Jack to the ends of the earth.

The Bells' friends did not desert them during this dreadful period. Every night there were at least four persons present, listening in horror and expostulating with the vile voices. The evening usually ended with

Blackdog threatening the other spirits with murder unless they desisted, and thrashing them if they refused to obey. On one occasion all four were beastly drunk, singing maudlin songs and filling the house with the stench of whiskey. They got it, Blackdog explained, at the still house of John Gardner, one of the neighbors.

Fortunately for Mr. Bell's sanity, this period did not last long. The witch family took to singing pious hymns instead of drinking songs, and finally departed, leaving "Kate"—the old familiar Spirit—in possession.

The inquirers never learned the answer to one of their questions. The Spirit did not explain its origin or give any clue as to how it could be dismissed. The second question—its purpose in coming—was answered. The Spirit was such a congenital liar that the inquirers failed to take this reply seriously at first, but in this, if in no other respect, it had told the simple truth. It had come to torment John Bell to death.

SIX

FROM THE DRUNKEN vulgarities of the witch family to the sweet singing of hymns, from malicious gossip to pious debates about religion, the Spirit displayed what may seem a striking inconsistency of character. Yet I venture to assert that it was no more inconsistent than most men or women, who are also susceptible to changes in personality—particularly when under the influence of liquor. If we examine its behavior, we will discover an underlying pattern.

From start to finish it was with the Bells for almost four years. I need not remind you, gentlemen, that this is one of the unique features of the case. Consider some of the implications. Through sheer familiarity the Bells came to regard the incredible presence as an old acquaintance—not one they would have cultivated by choice, perhaps, but no more vexatious in many ways than a grumpy, senile old relation. It is not surprising that after a year or two they accepted it with the same resignation they would have displayed toward any unmannerly human guest.

We must remember too that during this long period of time the mysterious voice was heard and investigated by dozens of people, some of them skeptical, educated men. Several of the Bells were suspected of fraud by investigators, but they were never caught. One visitor even clapped his hand over Betsy's mouth to see if this would inhibit the Spirit's voice. We can be sure that one or more of these skeptics would have proclaimed his triumph to the world if he had solved the mystery. None of them ever did.

I said that the Spirit demonstrated a certain consistency of personality, and this is nowhere better shown than in its attitude toward visitors. There were not dozens, but hundreds of these, most of them curiosity seekers who came from long distances to watch the show. Mr. Bell bore this with saintly patience, offering food and lodging to as many of the callers as he could accommodate, and never accepting a cent in payment. At times the Bell farm must have resembled a traveling circus, with carriages and wagons hitched to every fencepost, and tents covering the meadows.

The Spirit enjoyed company and seldom failed to perform. It put on some of its best shows for a certain mysterious "English gentlemen" mentioned by John Junior, who described him as "a high class man of great intelligence." Perhaps John had simply forgotten the gentleman's name; but he seems to hint at private reasons for keeping it a secret. If the Englishman really existed, he left no record of his encounters with the Spirit, although, according to John Junior, he stayed with the Bells for several months.

The most memorable of the Spirit's performances involved two of the ministers whom we have already met. This occurred on a Sunday evening, and both pastors had carried out their duties that morning. Reverend Fort had preached at the Baptist church, Reverend Gunn at the Methodist. The services both began at the traditional hour of eleven A.M., and the churches were some thirteen miles apart.

As the assembled company sat relaxing after the evening meal, the Spirit made its presence known and began questioning Reverend Gunn about certain fine points of doctrine in his sermon.

"How do you know what I preached about?" the astonished pastor inquired.

"I was there and heard you," was the reply. The voice then repeated the text, the sermon, and the closing prayer, in an excellent imitation of the preacher's very tones.

"Well," said one of the visitors jokingly, "Brother Fort has the advantage this time. The witch cannot criticize his sermon, since it was listening to Brother Gunn."

"Oh yes I can," said the Spirit.

"How do you know?"

"I was present and heard him." Whereupon followed an exact repetition of the Baptist minister's sermon, in his own voice.

None of the listeners ever forgot this tour de force. The visiting Englishman was treated to additional demonstrations of the Spirit's powers. One evening it claimed to have visited his far-off home and conversed with his family. It repeated the conversation, imitating the voices of the gentleman's mother and brother. Though the Spirit only wanted to assure the English family that their absent loved one was well and carry back any messages they might care to send, its visit was not a success. The gentleman's mother dismissed it with the remark that she had heard and seen enough, adding, "We do not want any more visits like that here."

Well, we can hardly blame her.

Not all the visitors came to be entertained. Some had hopes of solving the mystery. A certain Jack Busby, known as the Witch Killer, offered to destroy the Spirit with charmed silver bullets, a well-known weapon for dealing with evil spirits. The Bells welcomed him courteously, though I suspect that confirmed rationalist John Bell had little faith in Busby's boasts.

At first, however, the Witch Killer's presence seemed to intimidate the Spirit. Nothing was heard from it for a week. Busby claimed all the credit and prepared to leave, saying he had other business to attend to. "But," he added magnanimously, "I will return if the Witch comes back."

When he mounted his horse the animal rolled its eyes and refused to budge. Busby urged it on with kicks and cries, but to no avail. All at once the animal began to rear.

"I can make that horse go, old quack Busby," shouted the voice of the Spirit. "Let me get on behind."

The horse galloped off at full speed, while Busby desperately clutched his hat and fought to stay on. Needless to say, he did not return.

Another visitor, who called himself a "professional detective," had a different approach. The Bells had never seen or heard of this Mr. Williams until the day he walked into the house and offered his services, but they received him as they received everyone, with courtesy and open minds.

Williams was a portly, handsome man and a foppish dresser, but his manners were not so attractive as his appearance. After several days, during which time the Spirit was modestly silent, he informed another visitor that he had solved the mystery. As he had suspected, there was nothing supernatural about the case. The Bells were playing the tricks themselves, wanting a sensation—though why they should want something that deprived them of rest, privacy, and peace of mind he did not explain.

When Mr. Bell learned of the detective's theory, his indignation flared. He felt his hospitality had been violated and expressed his intention of evicting the slanderer.

"Never mind, Old Jack," said the Spirit. "I will take care of it."

So Mr. Bell said nothing. It was getting late, and he hated to throw a guest out into the dark with no other lodging close at hand. Besides, by that time he was well acquainted with the Spirit's methods, and he would not have been human if he had not rather looked forward to seeing the traducer "taken care of."

The Spirit bided its time until after the family had gone to bed. The house was so full of sightseers that Mrs. Bell had been forced to place straw mattresses on the floor of the reception room. The "professional detective" had one of these luxurious pallets to himself; he was too stout to share with anyone. No sooner had the lights been put out than the other guests heard unearthly cries from Williams. The Spirit was holding him down, pounding him, and cursing.

A candle was brought. The pounding stopped, but the Spirit's profane comments on Williams's character continued. The terrified detective spent the rest of the night sitting up in a chair with a lighted candle at his side. He left at daybreak, refusing the Bells' kind invitation to breakfast.

The most famous of the curiosity seekers was General Andrew Jackson, who had been John Junior's commander-in-chief at New Orleans. "Old Hickory" was no stranger to scandal; his violent temper had led to several duels, and his impetuous emotions had caused him to marry a lady before her divorce from her former husband was final.

The distinguished military man came with a large entourage and a wagon loaded with equipment. The cavalcade had almost reached the house when the horses came to a stop and could not be persuaded to move, though there was nothing impeding their progress.

"It's the witch," one of the party exclaimed.

From the bushes along the roadside a voice called, "All right. They can go on now, General."

And they did.

The Bells welcomed their honored guest and gave him a good dinner. There was no question of the General pitching a tent in the meadow; the best guest room was none too good for such a man. Before retiring, the company gathered around the fire, and we need not wonder what the subject of the conversation must have been.

One of the General's followers was in the same profession as Jack Busby—witch killing. He was a big man with fiery eyes and a hawklike nose. Like Busby, he relied on silver bullets. Boastfully he displayed his pistol and said he could hardly wait to try it out.

There was no comment from the Spirit, and the braggart's boasts grew louder. Jackson, never a patient man, began to fidget. He wanted some action. Suddenly the skeptic jumped up and grabbed the seat of his trousers.

"Boys, I am being stuck with a thousand pins," he yelled.

"I am in front of you," said a mocking voice. "Shoot."

The witch hunter drew his pistol, aimed it, and tried to pull the trigger. The weapon would not fire.

"It's my night for fun," the Spirit said, chuckling. The victim's head rolled from side to side and the sound of loud slaps was heard. Then, "It is pulling my nose off," screamed the witch hunter. He made a break for the door, which obligingly opened for him. As he ran screaming toward the wagon the voice jeered and hooted at him.

Jackson roared with laughter. "I have never heard or seen of anything so funny and mysterious," he exclaimed in delight. "I'd like to stay a week."

Though Mr. Bell must have resented being regarded as a source of entertainment, he assured his tactless guest that he was welcome to stay as long as he liked.

The Spirit was agreeable, too. "There is another fraud in your party, General," it commented. "I'll get him tomorrow night. It is getting late now; go to bed."

During the night General Jackson had a change of heart. One can hardly suspect the hero of New Orleans of being a coward, so it must have been someone else in the party who was afraid of being found out, and who persuaded the General to abandon the visit. However, he later admitted that he had felt a few qualms.

"By the Eternal, I saw nothing; but I heard enough to convince me that I'd rather fight the British than deal with this torment they call the Bell Witch."

SEVEN

N OW I WILL ADMIT, gentlemen, that these stories have a questionable air about them—an aura of the apocryphal, one might say. Yet they offer several important clues. Note, if you please, that some of the visitors came with the avowed intention of exposing the fraud, and that they failed to do so. Note also that in its treatment of the callers the Spirit was far from inconsistent. It reserved its jeers and slaps for the skeptics, and treated courteous visitor with courtesy.

The pattern is even clearer when we turn to its relations with close friends—I almost said "*its* close friends." Some of the Bells' neighbors got to be on excellent terms with the Spirit. It "enjoyed the gab," as the saying went, and was less apt to play nasty tricks when it was busy talking. Thus it was a true act of kindness for one of John Bell's friends to offer to chat with the Spirit for a few hours. The poor man probably took advantage of the peace and quiet to snatch a little sleep.

James Johnson, the first neighbor to make its acquaintance, was a particular favorite. Though it teased him and called him "Old Sugar Mouth," it acknowledged his admirable character. But James was not as entertaining as his son John, and the Spirit relished matching wits with this gentleman. John's character seems to have been well known to his neighbors; he put on a great show of candor and geniality, but he was not above using trickery to gain his ends. His brother Calvin, on the other hand, was without guile, a man of utter simplicity and honesty.

One evening the brothers were discussing some of the Spirit's antics with their hosts. Was it corporeal, but invisible? It must have hands; too many people had felt its hard slaps.

The Spirit chimed in. Yes, it had hands, would Calvin like to hold one of them, just for a moment?

Calvin certainly would.

"You must promise not to hold on, or squeeze it," warned the voice.

Calvin promised. He held out his hand.

The fingers that rested on his, shyly and fleetingly, were as soft and delicate as those of a woman.

A trifle miffed, John asked to be granted the same favor.

"You only want a chance to catch me," the Spirit said shrewdly.

"No, no, I promise."

"I know you, John Johnson. You are a grand rascal, trying to find me out, but I won't trust you."

So Calvin Johnson was the only person who ever felt the Spirit's touch—except for slaps and pinches. But another neighbor actually got his arms around it.

William Porter had spent night after night with the Bells in the hope of helping them. He and the Spirit were on good terms; it enjoyed his conversation almost as much as it did that of John Johnson. William, called Billy by his friends, was unmarried. His house was a typical bachelor log cabin, with only two rooms. There was a single fireplace at one end of the larger room. The second room was Billy's bedroom, and on cold nights he left his door open so the warmth of the fire could reach him.

One winter evening Billy arrived at the Bells to find a large company assembled, waiting for the Spirit to make an appearance. It was obvious that he was very excited, and he needed little persuasion to tell his story.

"It was a cold night last night, and I made a big log fire before retiring, to keep the house warm. As soon as I got in bed I heard scratching and thumping about the bed. Just like Kate's tricks, as I thought, but was not long in doubt as to the fact. Presently I felt the cover drawing to the back side, and immediately the witch spoke.

"'Billy, I have come to sleep with you and keep you warm.'

"'Well, Kate,' I replied, 'if you are going to sleep with me you must behave yourself.'

"I clung to the cover, feeling that it was drawing away from me, as it appeared to be raised from the bed on the other side, and something snakelike crawling under. I was never afraid of the witch, or apprehended that it would do me any harm; but somehow this produced a kind of chilly sensation, a freak of all-overishness that was simply awful. The cover continued to slip in spite of my tenacious grasp and was twisted into a roll on the back side of the bed, just like a boy would roll himself in a quilt, and not a strip was left on me. I jumped out of bed in a second, and observing that Kate had rolled up in the cover, the thought struck me, 'I have got you now, you rascal, and will burn you up.'

"In an instant I grabbed the roll of cover in my arms and started to the fire. It was very weighty and smelled awful. I had not gone halfway across the room before the luggage got so heavy and became so offensive that I was compelled to drop it on the floor and rush out of doors for a breath of fresh air. The odor emitted from the roll was the most offensive stench I ever smelled. It was absolutely stifling, and I could not have endured it another second.

"After being refreshed I returned to the room and gathered up the roll of bedclothing and shook it out, but Kate had departed and there was no unusual weight or offensive odor remaining. And that is just how near I came to catching the witch."

One of the Spirit's less attractive attributes was its vulgarly outspoken antipathy toward the family slaves. I will not comment at length on this barbaric custom, except to say that the relationship between master and slave on these western farms was quite different from the one that prevailed on the great eastern plantations, which might employ hundreds of persons. Mr. Bell worked closely with his slaves, many of whom had grown up in the family. Religious doctrine frowned on cruelty to slaves—though it condoned that greater injustice, slavery itself—and in that close-knit community a man could not mistreat his servants without the fact being known and censured by his peers. Slaveowners like the Bells viewed the servants with a kind of contemptuous affection. They cherished the fond delusion that their affection was returned, and perhaps, in some cases, it was. But beneath the seeming docility and the servile references to little Missy and dear old Massa must have boiled a sea of burning resentment.

The Spirit hated "niggers." This is a word the Bells would never have used, and in other ways the Spirit's behavior toward persons of the Negro race resembled that of the lowest and least educated classes in society. Being a social snob, it preferred the amenities of the master's house to the poor cabins of the slaves, and was never known to invade their quarters. But if one of the servants ventured outside after dark he might meet something he had not bargained for.

A young man named Harry, who was in his teens when the Spirit first appeared, lived to a ripe old age and was still working for the Bell family fifty years later. The children called him "Uncle Hack" and loved to listen to his stories of his encounter with the Spirit. We may be sure that these tales lost none of their dramatic content over the years.

One of Harry's chores was tending the fires, no light task when fireplaces were the only source of heat and wood was the only fuel. Like all young people, Harry liked to sleep late when he could get away with it. Winters in Tennessee can be chilly, and Mr. Bell was an early riser; it vexed him to rise from his warm bed and find that Harry had not started the fire.

He cannot have been a harsh master, for Harry was so unimpressed by the scoldings he received that he continued to sleep in. One morning he was very late. As he knelt by the hearth trying to blow the coals into flame, a piece of kindling rose into the air and applied itself to the seat of his trousers. Harry's attempts to avoid the missile were in vain. Invisible hands seized him, threw him across a chair, and smacked him harder than before. The sounds of the blows and the poor lad's cries were heard all over the house. John Bell came running. When the Spirit finally left off chastising the lad, he warned Harry that if he was late again he would be beaten to death and thrown into the fire.

We may be sure Harry was on time after that. In order to make his morning task easier, he carried in wood and kindling the night before. One night he was on his way to his cabin after finishing this chore when he heard the ominous voice address him from the darkness.

"Go right over to Mr. James Johnson's and cut wood and kindling for his morning's fires. He and his folks are sick, and I told him I would send you. James Johnson is the best man in this county. Your master will be glad I sent you; don't stop to ask him."

The Johnson house was half a mile away, and Harry must have been very tired. But he said he hurried—and I believe him. Mr. Johnson was expecting him. The Spirit had already spoken to him.

"It will be no trouble, Harry just likes to make fires on cold mornings," it said, with the sardonic humor it sometimes displayed. "If you are going to be sick long, Harry will come every day and see to your fires. I'll tell his master to send him and he will be glad to have it done."

Several of the other slaves felt the effect of the Spirit's disapproval, but it abused the members of the family even more.

The three younger boys, Joel, Richard, and Drew, all suffered from the Spirit's invisible hands. It pulled the covers off their beds, threw sticks and stones at them from the bushes along the road when they walked to school, slapped them and pulled their hair. Once when Drew was leaning against a heavy piece of furniture it yanked the support away from him so that he fell to the floor and bruised himself badly.

By contrast, the Spirit's behavior toward John Junior was curiously considerate. It never laid hands on him, and it addressed him in an almost apologetic manner. He was not at all afraid of it, and as its behavior worsened, he often threatened and cursed it. Once it admitted that it liked him because he had the courage to talk back to it.

"I will try to tell you of more pleasant things next time," it said, adding airily, "*au plaisir de vous revoir.*" We are told that the Spirit spoke all languages fluently, but this is the only specific example that has survived.

The Spirit, you see, had its amiable side. It was not an unmixed disaster for the Bells or for the neighborhood. Few examples of misbehavior went unnoticed, and it always reported these, in sanctimonious tones, to the chagrin of the parties concerned. Some of the neighbors ruefully admitted that the moral tone of the community had never been higher. A man who might be tempted to beat a slave or abuse his children would refrain, knowing that by nightfall everybody in the area would know about it. It must have been like having a policeman always at one's side.

For some of the Bells, however, its presence was far from pleasant. It never ceased to threaten Mr. Bell, and as the summer of 1819 approached, another of its purposes became apparent.

EIGHT

"Mid woodland bowers and grassy dell
Dwelt pretty blue-eyed Betsy Bell.
But elvin phantoms cursed the dell
And sylvan witches all unseen
Wielded scepter o'er this queen."

THE WOODCUT accompanying this bit of doggerel in a book written some years later does not flatter Miss Betsy. She resembles a witch herself, with her hair in wild disarray and her hands raised in horror. If she had been a lady of high degree in old Scotland (a region much afflicted with witchcraft, it seems), some Highland minstrel might have immortalized her sufferings in better verse, and a handsomer portrait might have been painted. But perhaps she was better off as she was. In a less enlightened age she might have been condemned for witchcraft, or sent some other poor wretch to a grisly death.

I told you Betsy was the heroine of this tale of Gothic horror, and I stick to that opinion, even though the Spirit itself is the major character. A good many clues suggest that it was of the female gender, but it is hard to ascribe sexual identity to a disembodied voice, and we cannot call the Spirit a heroine unless we are willing to apply the same term to characters like Medea and Messalina.

Betsy is certainly a central figure. Any theory that attempts to account for the strange happenings in the Bell household must focus on her, as victim or as perpetrator—and rest assured, she did not escape suspicion. What was she like, this queen of the dell?

Medical men may point out that Betsy was a child blossoming into womanhood, and therefore liable to be afflicted by female complaints common to that stage in life. But she was no swooning, civilized young lady. She was a healthy country girl, and something of a tomboy. "She knew all the trees, poplars, oaks, gums, maples, and all the others; she enjoyed the budding of the trees in the spring and loved their red and golden hues in the fall. She gathered the wild flowers and knew all the birds in the woodland."

This rhapsodic description was written half a century later by one of Betsy's partisans, in a period when flowery hyperbole was fashionable. It doesn't say much. Contemporary descriptions are more specific. Betsy was an excellent horsewoman. She could shoot a gun and hitch mules to a plow or wagon. "A stout girl," one of her brothers said approvingly. He was referring to her state of health, not to her figure; other witnesses describe her as blonde and lithesome, with a beautiful shape, a perfect complexion, and rosy lips, not to mention the blue eyes. She also possessed "good sense, a cheery disposition, and a perfect character."

More hyperbole! More revealing are Betsy's reminiscences when, as an old lady of eighty, she talked with her brother's grandson about her childhood days.

Memories of pleasure endure longer than memories of pain. Betsy's tales of her girlhood have an air of sunlit innocence that even the recurrent presence of the Spirit did not darken. Mr. and Mrs. Bell were not strict parents. They encouraged the young people in all sorts of harmless pleasures—picnics in the wood, fishing in the river, parties, horseback riding, evenings with friends. The Spirit enjoyed these activities, too. It seldom missed a party.

Sleigh riding was a popular winter sport. The vehicles were actually called slides, and were designed for farm work, the runners being cut from trees that had a natural curve. When mounted under a platform and carefully polished, they served to haul produce from the fields to the barns. In winter the rough vehicles made fine sleighs.

One sleigh ride proved a bit unusual. Betsy had invited a group of friends, both boys and girls, to spend the day, and after the usual hearty dinner, which was served at noontime, they decided to hitch up the sleigh and go for a ride. Bundled in coats and scarves and wool caps, the girls piled onto the slide while the boys went to get the horses. Suddenly a voice cried out, "Hold tight when we get to the corners," and off went the sleigh, sans horses. It went around the house three times, taking the corners so fast that the runners slipped and skidded and the girls squealed with mingled delight and fear.

The Spirit's presence proved helpful to the young people on several of their expeditions. It would advise them how to cast a line when they were fishing, and once it pulled an adventurous youth out of a pocket of quicksand. It also saved Betsy from death or serious injury on one occasion.

Betsy had gone for a ride with Richard and some of their friends, following the river to a bend where there were some magnificent poplar trees. Here they were caught by a sudden summer storm, but were unable to take shelter under the trees, for the high winds tore leaves and branches and even huge limbs away, and the youngsters were in danger of being struck. In an agitated voice the Spirit urged them to cross the river, where they would be safer, but the frightened horses refused to enter the water.

"You little fools," the Spirit cried. "Hold tight now and say nothing to the horses."

Calmed and led by invisible hands, the animals made the crossing. Later Betsy found the path they had left littered with great branches and fallen trees.

A curious and, I think, noteworthy footnote to this

tale is that Betsy insisted the Spirit had warned them not to go riding that day because a storm was approaching. She added, "It had a way of saying things like that when we were going off, just as our father did when he wanted us to stay home, and told us many things to scare us that were not true."

Need I point out to you gentlemen why I consider this comment significant? No, I see I do not.

Stories of the Spirit's kindly actions—there were others—all derived from stout old Mrs. Betsy herself after an interval of many years, give quite a different picture of the Spirit's interest in her than we get from other witnesses. According to her brothers and her friends, the invisible presence afflicted the girl more and more painfully as time went on.

Betsy began to suffer from fainting spells, as Richard calls them. In fact, they were a good deal more serious. After a period of panting and gasping, she would seem to stop breathing, and would remain unconscious for as long as half an hour. The seizures left no permanent effects, but they must have been agonizing to endure and dreadful to watch. No one doubted the Spirit was responsible for them. They came on in the evening, at about the time the Spirit usually presented itself, and while the girl was unconscious the voice was not heard.

As if this affliction were not enough, the Spirit now began a campaign to deprive Betsy of a young girl's fondest hope—a lover of her own.

Young as Betsy was, she had several admirers. Chief

among them was Joshua Gardner, the son of the neighbor who had unwittingly supplied the witch family with its whiskey. A picture of Joshua has survived; it shows he was a good-looking young chap, with regular features and a shock of thick dark hair. As soon as Joshua began to court the girl in earnest, the invisible chaperone made itself heard. At first its voice pleaded gently, "Betsy, please don't marry Joshua Gardner." Joshua and Betsy ignored the advice, so the Spirit took stronger measures. Not only did it resume its physical attacks on poor Betsy, yanking the combs from her thick yellow hair and slapping her face, but it abused the young couple verbally. One of the servants recalled overhearing one of these attacks when he was making up the fire in the room where the lovers were sitting:

"Lawd a mercy, I heard that Witch talk the awfullest 'fore them, just made Miss Betsy so shamed she had to rout out of the room, and that boy would go right on home."

One can't help wondering precisely what the Spirit said. It must have been vulgar in the extreme, for no one ever reproduced the remarks.

Joshua was not Betsy's only admirer. Another young man had watched her bloom into womanhood and had fallen helpless victim to her charms.

One of the admirable Mr. Bell's first projects on arriving in Tennessee was to build a schoolhouse on his property, not only for his own children but for any of the neighborhood youngsters who cared to attend.

Betsy was a student for four years, between the ages of ten and fourteen. As the young master, Richard Powell, watched her develop in beauty and intelligence he fell in love with her, but kept silent about his feelings. Her attachment to Joshua was known, and Richard may have felt he had nothing to offer. He was only a country schoolteacher, without prospects or property, and a good many years older than she.

Both her suitors were helpless witnesses of Betsy's sufferings at the hands of the Spirit. She had a champion, however—a neighborhood Hercules named Frank Miles. His feats of strength became proverbial. A neighbor recalled seeing him crack a black walnut between his teeth. This native American fruit, my friends, is not one of your paper-shelled almonds or pecans; its covering is as hard as a rock. I confess this feat impresses me more than any of the usual demonstrations of muscle power—though if I had been Mr. Miles's dentist, I would have advised him to show off in some other way.

Frank was a friend of Betsy's brother John and a constant visitor. Betsy said he thought of her as his little sister, but we may wonder whether this modest giant did not cherish warmer feelings for the golden-haired charmer. At any rate, he proclaimed himself her champion and did his best to overcome the slippery Spirit.

His first match with his elusive opponent was not a success. Frank was spending the night at the Bells, as he often did. The weather was freezing, so he was particularly annoyed when the covers started slipping off the bed. He grabbed one end of the quilt, and a regular tug-of-war ensued, which ended with the quilt being torn to pieces. When Frank lay down, the bed tick—a thin mattress—was pulled out from under him, and then the Spirit began striking him. No doubt its sneers and mocking laughter hurt Frank even more than the blows. "You're sure a strong man, Frank; you can knock the wind out of the air, but you're not dangerous in a tussle with a Spirit."

This was the first time Frank had been defeated in a trial of strength, and he resented it as much as he deplored the Spirit's treatment of Betsy. Once when Frank was visiting he told Betsy to come and sit by him.

"Nothing will bother you while I am present," he promised.

"You go home," the Spirit shrieked. "You can do no good here."

It proceeded to pull Betsy's hair so hard her combs fell to the floor, and it pinched her cheeks till they flamed.

Betsy's cavalier sprang to his feet, clenching his fists. "You are the biggest coward on earth to torture a child who is little more than a baby! Why not work on me, you fiend of Hell?"

As he exchanged threats and insults with the Spirit, Frank forgot his manners and used a few words gentlemen are supposed to suppress in the presence of a lady. The threats were useless; Frank learned that any attempt to defend the girl only made matters worse. He could only look at her sympathetically, and tell her she was bearing her trouble with the greatest courage in the world. Yes, I suspect Frank was another of Betsy's secret admirers, nor was she unmoved by his valor.

"I know he meant what he said," she remarked, in recounting the story, "when he offered to fight a fiend of Hell for the Bell family, even though he died on the spot."

Betsy has been regarded as one of the Spirit's chief victims; but I wonder. It certainly showed her kindness at times. To be sure, the slaps and tugging of hair can't have been comfortable, but they produced no serious injury, and the strange fainting spells may have been a side effect not directly caused by the Spirit. As for the broken romance—"the surrender of that most cherished hope that animates every young heart"—perhaps the Spirit was speaking the simple truth when it claimed Joshua would never make Betsy happy. We don't know what sort of man he was; in later life he may have been a drunkard or a wife beater—or just unsuited to Betsy.

NINE

I HAVE SPOKEN at length about slaves and children, about friends and visitors; but I have neglected one of the most important actors in this drama—Mrs. Lucy Bell.

I confess to a great deal of curiosity about this lady, but my curiosity must remain unsatisfied. No portraits of her have survived. Was she stout and gray-haired, like many a middle-aged mother of a large family, or was she slim and fair like her daughter? Did she have a weakness for fine clothes and lace trim on her aprons, or did she dress in sober brown? All we know about her is what her children and neighbors reported—she was the best of women. There could hardly be a more boring description! So let us turn to the sole unbiased witness—the voice that cursed Old Jack Bell and jeered at the children—the sardonic Spirit that invented mocking epithets even for persons it claimed to respect. Its comment on Mrs. Bell was short and succinct: "Old Luce is a good woman."

A cynic might say that she had to be good. She had no opportunity to be anything else. In those sober, God-fearing communities, far from the luxuries of urban culture, secular amusements were lacking, and a mature married lady had neither the time nor the inclination to join in the games proper to children. Lucy's religion provided her sole source of entertainment—if that word can be used for meetings devoted to prayer and Bible study and the advancement of missions.

Of course there were the quilting bees. You gentlemen may not be familiar with that peculiarly American institution, nor was I, until curiosity drove me to investigate it. The custom arose from the scarcity of cloth in a pioneer society. Every scrap was utilized, and the ingenious ladies learned to sew the fragments together in attractive patterns. Cold frontier nights made coverlets welcome; the bright quilts, filled with an additional layer of material to increase their warmth, were a vital part of the household linen. They had another quality which was just as important: they provided an outlet for the love of beauty which is one of humanity's more admirable attributes. Heaven knows these women needed some such vent, deprived of luxury by their stern lives and forbidden vanity by their preachers. As time went on, the patterns became more elaborate, and the stitches that held the scraps together took on a baroque intricacy.

Quilting could be a solitary activity, but it went much faster when a number of people worked together, and who can blame these women for taking advantage of an opportunity to socialize? There is a sentimental charm in our mental pictures of these gatherings: the ladies in their modest gowns, gathered around the wide wooden frame on which the cloth was stretched, their full skirts billowing around them, their heads bent over their flashing needles. I wonder if you sense, as I do, the sinister currents in this harmless pastime? For who knows, gentlemen, what women talk about when they are alone? What thoughts burgeon behind the smooth white brows and issue from the demure, smiling lips?

A mere man hardly dares speculate. The ladies, of course, would have us believe their conversation was as innocent as their work. Perhaps they exchanged recipes and household hints, boasted of their husbands' success and the beauty and intelligence of their children. No doubt there were references to certain subjects modest females would not discuss in the presence of men. But was that all? Gossip, gentlemen, gossip! Some of it innocent enough—Mrs. Jones's new gown, the Smiths' visitors from Virginia. I venture to suggest, however, that the news was not always so innocuous. Who knows what rumors of violence and cruelty, or legal crime and moral sin, were whispered across the quilting frame?

With these suggestions in mind, you will not be surprised to learn that the Bell Spirit was an enthusiastic participant in Mrs. Bell's quilting parties. Its propensity for gossip has suggested to some analysts that it was female, but I would not be guilty of suggesting that love of malicious talk is limited to the gentler sex.

On the whole the Spirit behaved well at these times, out of respect for Mrs. Bell. Sometimes it would sing lovely melodies, unfamiliar to the awed group of ladies—"but all agreed they were sacred hymns." Sometimes, however, it regaled the ladies with rude and humorous stories about their husbands. This doesn't prove it was female; it proves only that it was adept at talking about subjects that would interest its audience. Do not doubt, gentlemen, that our wives might listen with faint, sly smiles to tales that mock our folly, just as we sometimes joke about their charming illogic.

We can be sure that while the Spirit was in residence, quilting parties at the Bells' were extremely popular. Kate the witch knew everything that went on in the neighborhood and had no hesitation about telling tales. There was no shame in listening; the ladies might have scorned to repeat such scandal themselves, but how could they control the tongue of an invisible spirit, or question its supernatural knowledge?

Lucy Bell was afraid of the strange entity and tried not to antagonize it. "She always spoke kindly of it and to it, thus hoping in some measure to influence a better treatment for her two loved ones, her husband and her daughter." In this she did not succeed, but in every other way the Spirit repaid her with consideration and with assistance. It kept her informed about her family in North Carolina, told all the news about her neighbors (including some news the subjects would have preferred to keep quiet), and gave her useful advice on household matters.

Why the tender consideration for Lucy Bell? Her children and neighbors asked themselves the same question. The only answer they could come up with was that Lucy's pious, saintly character gave her immunity from demonic spirits. This Spirit was always ready to acknowledge genuine goodness; though it made fun of "Old Sugar Mouth," it called him a good man and sent Harry to cut wood for him when he was ill. It argued theology with the preachers, but told the members of their flocks that they were fortunate to have such fine men as spiritual leaders.

However, this interpretation is not really convincing. For if true kindness and virtue rendered an individual safe from the Spirit, what are we to think about Mr. Bell, who was tormented and reviled? Nothing in the record hints at evil-doing on his part. I myself have developed a respectful affection for this upright old man. I am not impressed by the conventional praise offered by his children and friends, but I am struck by his behavior throughout the whole dreadful affair. His reverence for the Indian graves and his stout defence of old Mrs. Kate Batts show him to have been an admirable human being. Why should such a man be tormented to death, as was the Spirit's avowed aim?

No doubt you all have explanations, as do I. But first let us see how the doom of John Bell was carried out.

TEN

IT WAS IN THE SPRING of 1820 that events began to hasten toward their tragic end. Mr. Bell's torment had begun long before, but until the Spirit claimed responsibility he attributed his pains to natural causes. He was seventy years old, and despite the fact that he was a big, healthy man, some infirmities were to be expected.

Yet his initial symptoms were of a peculiar nature, and they increased in severity as time went on. At times his tongue would swell so that it filled his mouth, making speech or eating impossible for a day at a time. The sensation of a sharp stick laid crosswise in his mouth became more frequent. Gradually other symptoms developed—spasms of the muscles of his face, uncontrollable twitching and tics. As her father's suffering increased, Betsy's diminished. Her "fainting spells" had virtually disappeared by the summer of 1820.

Mr. Bell was much worse. An alarming increase in the severity of his muscular spasms was accompanied by a spate of abuse from the Spirit, whose violent threats and foul language were so bad that no one could bring himself to repeat them. Mr. Bell had already sought the advice of the family doctor, Dr. Hopson. Now his friends persuaded him to seek the advice of a specialist.

Dr. Mize lived in Simpson County, Kentucky, about thirty-five miles away. His title is misleading. He was no physician, but a conjurer, magician, and medicine man. Let us not sneer at poor John Bell for consulting such an obvious quack; all natural means had failed him, and he was beginning to realize his life was in danger. Persuaded by his friend James Johnson and his son Drew, he agreed to give the magician a trial, and Drew and Mr. Johnson set off to fetch him. They left at three A.M., in order to get out of the neighborhood before the Spirit turned up at its usual hour in the morning.

The journey was kept a profound secret, and this rather naive tactic seems to have puzzled the Spirit at first. When it realized Drew was not at home, it demanded to know where he had gone. Baffled in its enquiries—for John Bell was not inclined to give the secret away, and no one else knew the truth—it disappeared for the rest of the day.

Later that evening it joined the family in the reception room. It was in triumphant good spirits.

"I got on their track," it crowed. "Drew and Old Sugar Mouth—I overtook them twenty miles on the way and hopped in the road before them, looking like a poor sick old rabbit. Old Sugar Mouth knew me. 'There is your witch, Drew,' he said. 'Take her up in your lap. Don't you see how tired she is?'"

The Spirit had discovered the reason for Drew's absence, but it did not attempt to halt the mission. The travelers finished their journey and found Dr. Mize at home. After hearing their story he informed them that the case was a particularly difficult and unusual one. Mr. Bell was under a curse—that was the problem. However, he was confident he could remove the spell. As soon as he had finished his other jobs, he would visit the Bells.

Ten days later, Dr. Mize duly arrived. He got to work at once, searching the house for evidence of witchcraft. Triumphantly he pounced on an old shotgun that had been inoperative for some time.

"The witch has put a curse on it," he declared.

After some spells and conjuration—and some cleaning and repairs—lo and behold, the shotgun worked as well as ever.

The repair of the gun was the conjurer's major accomplishment during the three days following his arrival, but he did a lot of bragging about his former successes. Mr. Bell was not impressed; one look at Dr.

Mize had convinced him the man was a humbug. But Mize insisted he was on the way to solving the case. Had he not taken the curse off the gun? Had not the witch been quiet since he came?

The family knew better. They had seen the Spirit deal with skeptics and know-it-alls before.

It is difficult not to side with the Spirit in this instance, as we read Richard Bell's description of the magician in action—drawing pentagrams on the parlor floor, intoning weird spells in a sepulchral voice, and cooking up noxious messes of horrid-smelling potions. While he was engaged in his gyrations a voice inquired, "What the devil do you think you are doing with all that hocus-pocus?"

The startled seer whirled around, rolling his eyes wildly from side to side in an attempt to locate the source of the impertinent voice. But no man can acquire a reputation as a magician without having a cool head and a smooth tongue. Mize soon recovered himself and questioned the Spirit. He was no match for this diabolical debater, who had outargued cleverer men than Mize. After an exchange of questions, the Spirit lost its temper and began to swear in earnest. Its command of profanity must have been superb. Mize had unquestionably been cursed before, but this verbal blast scared him so badly he decided he had better leave. He did not escape without a final gesture from the Spirit, who made his horse buck and then bolt, with the terrified sorcerer clinging to its mane.

This admittedly comic episode—low comedy though it is—was the only light moment in an affair that rapidly went from bad to worse. John Bell's suffering intensified, and in September Mrs. Bell also became ill.

It is a wonder this much-tried woman had not long since succumbed to nervous prostration, but the Spirit could not be blamed for her illness, even indirectly. It was diagnosed as pleurisy, and of all the visitors who came to comfort the sick woman, none was so assiduous as the Spirit.

"Luce, poor Luce," it exclaimed, in tones of plaintive and touching sweetness. "I am so sorry you are sick. Don't you feel better, Luce? What can I do for you?"

"I am too sick to talk to you now," Lucy replied feebly.

The voice immediately fell silent and remained so while Lucy tried to rest. As is normal in this disease, she was most feverish and uncomfortable in the late afternoon and evening. She usually got some rest in the latter part of the night and woke refreshed in the morning. As soon as she opened her eyes, the anxious voice asked, "How do you feel this morning, Luce? Did you rest well through the night?'

Despite this concern, Mrs. Bell gradually grew worse. The family feared she was dying, and the Spirit became absolutely frantic with worry. It was particularly concerned about Lucy's appetite, or lack thereof. One day, in the same plaintive voice, it asked, "Luce, poor Luce, how do you feel now? Hold out your hands, Luce, and I will give you something."

Obediently Lucy cupped her hands. Into them fell a rain of hazelnuts, apparently originating from the empty air above the bed.

The ladies who were visiting the sick woman exclaimed in astonishment. One of them climbed on a chair to examine the ceiling, but found not even a crack through which the nuts could have been dropped.

"Say, Luce, why don't you eat the nuts?" the Spirit demanded.

"I cannot crack them."

"Well, I will crack some for you."

Cracking sounds were distinctly heard before the fragments of nuts dropped into the bed.

"Eat the nuts, they will do you good," the voice insisted.

"You are so kind," Lucy said tactfully. "But I am too sick to eat them."

So the next offering was a bunch of grapes, which appeared on her bedside table before the startled eyes of Reverend Fort and his son, who had come to pray for the sufferer. Lucy was unable to eat these either, but expressed her thanks, and from this time, twenty days after the attack began, she steadily improved until she was out of danger.

The delighted Spirit lavished praise on Dr. Hopson, the family physician; and I think that we must also give the credit for Mrs. Bell's recovery to this practitioner, for the Spirit seems to have been singularly inept in cases of sickness. Not only was it unable to help Mrs. Bell by supernatural means, but it was not very good at providing food a sick person could relish. Nuts and grapes were in season and were easily procured from the woods, but they are not necessarily what the doctor would order for an invalid.

As the wife improved, the husband grew worse. In mid-October Mr. Bell had a severe attack. He stayed in bed for almost a week, the Spirit cursing and threatening him all the while. On the morning of the twentieth he felt better, so he woke Richard and asked the boy to accompany him to the hog pens, in order to separate the stock hogs from the animals designated to be fattened for slaughter.

They had not gone far before one of Mr. Bell's shoes was jerked off his foot. Richard put his father's shoe back on, drawing the laces as tight as possible and tying a double knot. Mr. Bell started out again. It had not rained for several days, and the ground was dry and smooth. But after a few steps Mr. Bell's other shoe flew off.

The courageous old gentleman persevered. He and his son reached the pen and did what they had come to do. No sooner had they started back to the house than the insane performance began again. Mr. Bell's shoes flew off his feet. His body jerked and twitched in frightful convulsions, while the crisp autumn air rang with the derisive laughter and vulgar songs of the Spirit.

For the first and last time Richard saw his father break down. Tears streamed from his eyes as he told his son he feared his time had come.

With Richard's help Mr. Bell finally reached the house. There they were met by John Junior, who ran to their assistance, horrified at his father's appearance.

"His shoestrings were broken, his feet had bleeding gashes on them, his face was livid in spots, as from blows. His eyes were red and watery, as though he had received punches in both eyes. His face was contorted and twitching; he still complained of pain all over his face, in his eyes and about his head."

Richard was almost incoherent with shock, but he managed to give his older brother an account of what had happened, and the two young men helped their father into bed. Then John ran out of the house. Lifting his hands to heaven, he knelt in prayer.

"Send back this demon and give me a chance to return the same cruel punishment it has given Father. As a man, unaided by divine power, I cannot cope with this demon. Give me this aid, I beg you!"

But there was no response from the empty blue heavens, and the Spirit prudently kept silent.

Mr. Bell never left the house again. Dr. Hopson prescribed various medicines; we are not told what kind, nor do we know what other methods, if any, the physician employed. In all fairness to Dr. Hopson, we must remember that medical knowledge was extremely primitive. There was very little he could do, and by this time the doctor, the family, and John Bell himself had probably resigned themselves to the will of God—or the will of something. The Spirit claimed full responsibility; it continued to crow and congratulate itself, and revile "old Jack Bell."

Sick as he was, Mr. Bell had tried to keep up his old habit of being the first to rise in the morning. On December nineteenth he did not waken. The family was glad to see him getting some rest. His wife slipped quietly out of the room to superintend the preparation of breakfast, and John and Drewry went to feed the stock—the first order of business on a working farm, never to be neglected in spite of illness or bad weather.

After breakfast the boys looked in on their father again. He was still asleep. But alarm replaced their relief as they looked closer. Mr. Bell was not sleeping, he was in a coma, and all attempts to rouse him failed.

The doctor was sent for, and John, who had been in charge of administering his father's medicine, went running to the cupboard. When he opened it, "The three bottles of medicine which I had been giving him were gone. In their place was a dark bottle containing a brown smoky fluid which I had never seen before."

By this time the family's closest neighbors and friends had arrived, Frank Miles and John Johnson among them. John called them to look at the mysterious bottle. None of them had seen it before.

"The damned witch did this," Frank exclaimed with his customary bluntness.

The Spirit promptly confirmed the accusations. "I did it. Old Jack will never get up from that bed again. I have got him this time!"

Dr. Hopson arrived and joined the others at Mr. Bell's bedside. He shook his head gravely. John showed him the bottle. As he examined it, the Spirit cried out, "I put it there, and gave Old Jack a big dose out of it last night while he was fast asleep, which fixed him."

"I certainly did not leave it here," the doctor muttered. "Nor can I tell what it contains. Perhaps we should test it."

The test was unfortunately typical of the medical procedures of that day and that remote region. One of the barn cats was caught, and a straw was dipped into the brown liquid and wiped across its tongue.

The cat jumped and whirled over a few times, stretched out, kicked, and died.

In a passion of anger and frustration, John threw the fatal bottle into the fire. A flash of light and a blue flame marked its destruction.

As the sun declined, John Bell's family sat by his bed watching helplessly as he sank deeper into unconsciousness. Their sad vigil was enlivened by the loathsome voice singing vulgar songs and preening itself on its crime. Early in the morning of December twentieth, two months to the day since the attack at the hog pen, John Bell breathed his last.

His funeral drew the largest crowd ever seen at such occasions in Robertson County. The air was bright and crisp that morning, only a few days before Christmas. John Bell's grave had been dug on the hill under the tall cedars, beside the resting place of his son Benjamin. Mrs. Bell's somber black gown and muffling widow's veil absorbed the chilly sunlight. As the mourners turned away, the clods of earth falling onto the coffin rang hard as stones. Then, from the empty air, came the Spirit's epitaph on the man it had murdered.

"Row me up some brandy, O!" it sang, and continued with the raucous drinking song until the family had entered the house.

> *"Row me up some brandy, O*
> *Row, row, row*
> *Row me up some brandy, O.*
> *Row me up some more."*

The Bells' Christmas that year cannot have been merry.

As the bleak winter days passed, Mrs. Bell found a few rays of light in the gloom of her bereavement. She had strong sons to carry on her husband's work, and many loyal friends. The Spirit's worst malice had apparently been expended on John Bell; it had never been rude or unpleasant to Lucy, and that winter it was even kind to Betsy, bringing her exotic delicacies to tempt her failing appetite, and telling her amusing stories about social events in the outside world. As might have been expected of so shallow a personality, most of these tales concerned the doings of the wealthy and socially prominent, in Europe and in America. The newspapers took some time to reach that remote region, but when they arrived Betsy found the Spirit's descriptions of balls and parades—and scandals—completely accurate.

In those salubrious climes spring comes early. The first wildflowers bloom amid the snows of February, and April sees the forest floor carpeted with violets. Betsy's young heart bloomed as well. She was now seventeen years old—the tenderest, most beautiful age of a woman's life. Handsome gray-eyed Joshua was at her side, and it was spring. But when Joshua proposed marriage she held back. Her forebodings were justified. The Spirit had not abandoned its unexplained opposition to the young man, and one day, when Josh pleaded his suit in passionate language, he was interrupted by the old refrain: "Betsy, don't marry Joshua Gardner!"

Once again brother John was consulted—at least, that is what John claimed. The Spirit demanded that he intervene to prevent the marriage. As before, it refused to give reasons, but John took Betsy aside for a private talk. Neither of them ever divulged what he said (indeed, Betsy never mentioned it at all), but evidently John warned his sister of the peril she was facing. That same day Betsy told Joshua she could never be his.

Many years later, after a long and happy life, Betsy looked back on this decision and expressed considerable resentment—not of the Spirit, but of friends who had criticized her for not defying the eerie voice. She claimed they had no right to judge her, for they had never been in her position—and indeed, few women have. Over and over the Spirit had proved its power to hurt and harm. Should she have exposed her lover to the malice that had already destroyed her father? It would not have been fair to Joshua.

This last concession satisfied the Spirit. Though it lingered on for several months, its tricks gradually decreased in frequency. One night as the family sat around the fire, an object like a cannonball rolled down the chimney and out into the room, bursting into a great cloud of smoke.

"I am going," the odiously familiar voice announced. "I will be gone for seven years. Good-bye to all."

ELEVEN

THE SPIRIT had indeed departed. The years passed and the old house saw the usual changes, including several weddings. Yes, Betsy was a bride—but her favored suitor was not Josh Logan. Perhaps she feared the Spirit would return prematurely if she violated its command. Or perhaps there were other reasons. Who can fathom the mysteries of a young girl's heart?

Betsy's husband was Richard Powell, the schoolmaster. He waited a decent interval—whatever that may be—after Joshua's dismissal before expressing his love. By then he had entered the state legislature and was something of a catch. The fact that he was considerably older than his bride was unimportant; as brother John sagely remarked, a good marriage consists of "a husband taking all the ills

BARBARA MICHAELS

of life to himself and not allowing her to assume respon-
sibilities which might become burdensome." The marriage lasted only seventeen years, but by all accounts it
was a happy one.

Drewry had bought a farm across the river from his
father's and lived alone with only his slaves for company. His nature was not so resilient as his sister's. His
father's dreadful death had left memories from which he
never recovered, and he lived in constant fear of the
Spirit's return.

John Junior was also living alone on his own property. In 1828 he brought home a bride, one of the daughters of the Methodist minister Thomas Gunn. However,
he was still unmarried in February of that year when the
Spirit, true to its promise, paid its second visit.

The family had never doubted that it would return.
At that time only three of the Bells remained in the old
home—Mrs. Lucy Bell and her youngest sons, Richard
and Joel.

It came as it had come the first time, signalling its
presence by scratching on the outside walls of the
house, then moving inside, scraping and rapping and
tugging at the bedclothes. Richard, sleeping alone in his
former room, was the first to sense the Spirit's presence.
Courageously he kept silent, hoping the unwelcome
visitor would give up and leave. A few nights later, however, he heard sounds from the next room, where his
mother and his brother Joel were sleeping, and knew
his hopes were vain.

Lucy and the boys talked the matter over and decided the best course was to ignore the manifestations. Perhaps they had put two and two together—on its first visit the Spirit had not spoken until it was spoken to. The strategy was effective. Two weeks of comparatively minor disturbances followed. Then they stopped altogether. The Spirit had not spoken a single word. But it had not departed. Little did the rejoicing survivors know that it had merely found a more receptive host.

John Bell Junior had been one of the Spirit's most outspoken antagonists. He had berated and cursed it, he had offered to take on himself the sufferings of his sister and his father. It had suffered his threats with remarkable humility, so perhaps it is not surprising that on its second visit it should prefer his company to that of his mother and younger brothers. What does surprise us is how the entity had changed in seven years.

One March evening, as John sat reading in his study, came a voice long unheard but instantly recognized.

"John," it began meekly, "I hope you will not be as angry with me on this visit as you were on my last. I shall do nothing to cause you offense; I have been in the West Indies for seven years, and—"

"Wherever you have been, or whatever you are, your proper place is in Hell," John said angrily.

"There are thousands of human beings now living on this earth who are worse than I," the Spirit protested. "If their spirits could return to earth they would raise a thousand times more Hell than I have done."

John replied with a scorching denunciation. "I would give my life freely," he cried dramatically, "if I could grasp your form in my arms and crush you slowly, giving you the pain you caused my father scores of times, and then throw you straight into the fires of Hell."

Unmoved by John's threats, the Spirit returned on successive nights. The two bizarre companions had long conversations. The Spirit told John that there would be a great war between the states, to free the slaves. Though it was not fond of the Negro race, it felt it would be better to free them. It also predicted a war between nations, into which the United States would be drawn. There was danger of a second dreadful world conflict, which, "if it comes," would be worse than the first. Besides predicting these and other disasters—floods, earthquakes, drought—the Spirit entertained John with long, tedious descriptions of Heaven and Hell, the pre-Adamic history of mankind, and the nature of Jesus Christ. I regret to say that although its command of English had improved considerably, with no trace of the bad grammar and vulgarities that had marred its earlier conversation, it had acquired a literary style both pompous and imprecise. I will therefore spare you further quotations.

After several months the Spirit announced that its visit the following evening would be its last. "But," it said, "I will return again in one hundred years plus seven."

"That was the last we ever saw or heard of the Spirit," John told his son, the only person to whom he ever spoke of his incredible experiences. Of all the Spirit's remarks, the one that impressed him most was its "almost eyewitness accounts" (whatever that ambiguous description may mean) of the Crucifixion and death of Christ. John refused to repeat this even to his son. "It was too heartrending for me to call it to your mind. My life has been so saddened by this recital of the terrible torture of our Saviour that I can never get over it."

But was this really the end of the Bell Witch? By no means. It had promised to return in a hundred years plus seven. The promised date was 1935.

TWELVE

SHORTLY AFTER the Spirit's second visit, Mrs. Lucy Bell was laid to rest beside her husband in the quiet graveyard on the hill. After her death no one cared to live in the house that had seen so many strange and terrible events. Gradually it decayed and at last was torn down. Except for Drewry, whose existence was lonely and fearful, the children of John Bell Senior lived long and prospered. Indeed, one might suspect that instead of being a family bane, the Spirit had brought them good fortune. John Junior succumbed to pneumonia at what was, for the Bells, the early age of sixty-nine. If he had taken better care of himself he might have enjoyed the life span given to his brother Joel—seventy-seven—and his sister Betsy—eighty-six. Several of the friends who had worn away so many evenings debating with the Spirit also lived to remarkable ages. Thomas Gunn, the Methodist minister, was ninety-six when he died, but he was outdone by Old Sugar Mouth, James Johnson, who missed the century mark by a single year.

The surviving members of the family resented the notoriety the Spirit had brought and refused to discuss the matter except, rarely, with close kin and friends. The only one to put the tale in writing was Richard. His diary is said to have been composed in 1846, but he refused to have it published, though many interested parties applied for permission to do so. Only after the last member of that generation had passed on did Richard's son Alan Bell give the manuscript to a newspaperman of Clarksville, Mr. M. V. Ingram. Ingram's book was published in 1894. In addition to Richard's recollections, it included letters and interviews with neighbors. Few of the eyewitnesses were still living; most of Ingram's correspondents were their sons and daughters, who had heard the stories told by their parents. One or two of the chapters are obviously pure imagination, embroidered by Mr. Ingram in the fulsome and flowery style of that time—it would make Sir Arthur wince to hear it.

Meanwhile, gossip and rumor had not been idle. Skeptics selected Betsy Bell as the perpetrator of the tricks, though none actually went so far as to accuse her of killing her father. Others suggested that the two older boys, John Junior and Drewry, had learned "magic arts" such as ventriloquism during their journeys to New Orleans, and had helped their little sister deceive the rest of the family. In 1849 the *Saturday Evening Post* published an article which suggested this theory. But they underestimated Mrs. Betsy. She brought a lawsuit, and the *Post* was forced to retract its innuendoes.

As time passed the story was more or less forgotten, except in Robertson County and in the section of Mississippi to which descendants of the Bells had migrated. Told and retold, embroidered and misinterpreted, it took on elements of a classic ghost story, with very little remaining of the original facts.

In Tennessee to this very day the "Bell Witch" Cave is a local tourist attraction, and residents regale credulous psychic investigators with solemn lies about the Witch's most recent capers.

The Bells themselves had preserved in writing and in family tradition a closer version of the truth. How close we will never know, for Ingram's edition of Richard Bell's diary was not published until almost seventy years after the Spirit's departure. Forty years after that, another member of the Bell family, Dr. Charles Bailey Bell, took pen in hand to write about the "family trouble." It is from these two volumes that I have drawn most of the facts—and fictions—I have narrated this evening, ignoring the wilder tales passed on by persons not directly involved.

Dr. Bell, a physician and specialist in nervous disorders, was the grandson of John Junior. In 1934 he was sixty-four years old. Since boyhood he had heard tales of the witch from Uncle Hack (formerly Harry), Frank Miles, and other eyewitnesses. As a young man of nineteen he paid a visit to his great-aunt Betsy and listened to her reminiscences. His father, Joel Thomas Bell, son of John Junior, passed on in 1910, but before he died he told Charles about John's philosophical discussions with the Spirit. Dr. Charles must have been steeped in the story for decades. He was convinced that the Spirit would keep its promise to return, and that he would be the one it visited.

In 1934 he wrote his book, explaining in the introduction why he felt it necessary to publicize matters which the family had kept private so long. He believed the country and the world were in desperate straits. Though this is not an uncommon attitude for conservative old gentlemen to hold, he had some reason for pessimism. The United States was gripped by Depression. Europe was in turmoil. Adolf Hitler was Chancellor of Germany. Godless Communism reigned in Russia. Religion was dying. One might ask how the bizarre antics of a century-old ghost could assist the troubled world, which had problems enough without speculating on the supernatural. Dr. Charles had the answer. In its long and tedious conversations with his grandfather, the Spirit had testified to the divinity of Jesus Christ and the truth of the Christian faith.

The Spirit's religious views, like its philosophy, are too tedious to bear repetition. Whether they are to be attributed to the good doctor himself, or to his grandfather, or to a combination thereof, I would not venture to say, but I feel sure they did not come from the vulgar raucous thing, whatever it was, that had followed John Bell to his grave singing drinking songs.

Not that I believe for an instant that Dr. Bell set out deliberately to deceive. But we should note that by the 1930s many of the events the Spirit had predicted so accurately were a matter of history, and that war clouds were gathering again over Europe. The good doctor believed the family Spirit would come to him in 1935. He was disappointed. It came not to him, nor, so far as we know, to any other member of the family. The "Bell Witch" had finally been laid to rest.

THIRTEEN

WHEN HOUDINI FINISHED, the air was gray with smoke and the glasses were empty. The stranger, who had displayed signs of increasing restlessness during the last part of the narrative, could contain himself no longer.

"Why, gentlemen, what a pack of nonsense! It is obvious that the true explanation—"

"Wait." Fodor wagged an admonishing forefinger. "We will hear your explanation in due course, my dear sir; it is in the hope of obtaining a fresh viewpoint that we did ourselves the honor of inviting you to be present this evening. But, with your permission, we would like to keep you to the last—for a sweet, as it were. Let us first present our own theories of what the Bell Witch really was. Will you go first, Frank? I'll wager most of us can predict what you are going to say. Another naughty little girl, eh?"

Podmore's thin lips curved. He leaned forward, hands clasped, and began.

FOURTEEN

PODMORE:
THE NAUGHTY LITTLE GIRL

FIRST, GENTLEMEN, let me perform a service for all of us and clear away some of the deadwood that has accrued to this case. We are to examine the evidence. What can be considered evidence, and what pure imagination?

One of our rules—a basic rule of any investigation—is to suspect any tale that rests on the statement of a single witness. On this basis, if on no other, we can throw out most of the evidence of the family servants. Many of Mrs. Betsy's tales fall into the same category. Particularly absurd is her story of the supernatural sleigh ride. Yes, I fear that in her dotage the old lady let her fancy wander freely. As for John Junior's conversations with the Spirit—out the window with them all. It matters not whether we attribute them to John or to his descendants; they are palpable falsehoods. Recall that the only time the Spirit, who is supposed to have known all languages, actually used a foreign phrase, it was to John Junior—and it was French, a language he alone knew.

Yet after all the nonessentials are stripped away we must admit that something invaded the Bell home in the spring of 1817. It was heard to speak by hundreds of witnesses. Its attacks on Betsy were seen by dozens. That is the core of the story, and a fact for which we must account.

Fodor is pleased to jest about my naughty little girl. Never let me be accused of bias against the fair sex, gentlemen; often the culprit is a naughty little boy. In this case, though, Miss Betsy must stand in the dock.

As you know, I have personally investigated numerous cases of poltergeists and haunted houses. In almost all of them the center of the disturbance was a child or a mentally retarded adult. I have been accused of being unfair to these unfortunates; so, instead of giving you an example from my own experience, let me make my point by quoting a case in which I was not involved. It took place in a small town in Berkshire, in 1895. The investigator was Mr. Westlake, one of our most experienced agents. It was, on the face of it, a typical poltergeist case. For several weeks the family had experienced outbursts of mysterious activities. Furniture darted around the room; burning coals shot out of the fireplace; sticks, teapots, and cups flew through the air.

Mr. Westlake went to Berkshire with an entirely open mind. The first day he saw nothing, but attributed the inactivity of the poltergeist to the factor called "witness inhibition" by some of my colleagues. They claim that the presence of an outsider, particularly a skeptic, puts a damper on the poltergeist's ability to perform. Well, it does, but not for the reason they think.

Westlake observed that the parents, Mr. and Mrs. Turner, were genuinely puzzled and distressed. So was one of the children, a boy, who does not enter into this story. The other child, dwarfish little dark-haired Polly, said little at first; she sat in the chimney corner cuddling her two cats.

Later that day Mr. Westlake wrote as follows: "'The Ghost is a humbug now, whatever it may have been. I made friends with the cats, and their mistress, poor child, gave me a private sitting of some two or three hours, in the course of which she moved between forty and fifty objects when she thought I wasn't looking. On at least seven occasions I had a clear view of her hands in contact with the objects, and saw them quickly moved."

This case is so typical of others I have encountered that I consider it offers the true explanation of the so-called poltergeist. Naive persons believe a mere child would be physically incapable of engineering the effects, and too sweet and innocent to worry her family in such a way. Balderdash, gentlemen—or, as Houdini might say, "Bunk!" Children aren't angels, they are human beings at a particularly troubled time of life. Resenting the control exercised over them by adults, they are too weak to fight back and too helpless to escape. No wonder they enjoy seeing the big bullies who rule them frightened and confused! As for the skill necessary, that too is a fallacy, though I admit one has to see the little dears at work before one can believe how devilishly clever they are.

Miss Betsy's lissome, twelve-year-old form flitted noiselessly along the dark halls of that isolated house, tugging at her brothers' hair, scratching and rapping and growling like a dog. The absence of artificial lights made the production of uncanny noises and whispering voices childishly simple. How often, in the narrative, did you notice the phrase "when the lights were brought in"? The phenomena ceased when a candle was lit.

Particularly significant is the story of the nuts and grapes presented to Mrs. Bell when she was sick in bed. Whose room was it that was directly over Mrs. Bell's? The fruits were in season in the nearby woods. The evidence of the witnesses, that there was no crack or hole in the ceiling above the bed, doesn't count for a jot. How on earth were ladies in their tight corsets and full skirts to climb up far enough to make sure there were no loose boards?

Betsy didn't want to marry Joshua Gardner. Perhaps

her parents were urging her; perhaps Joshua was becoming too insistent, and Betsy had her eye on the young schoolmaster. Why not use the monster she had created to rid her of the nuisance? Self-inflicted injuries are common in cases of fraud and hysteria. The little victim shrieks, "Ah, it is slapping me!"—claps her hands to her cheeks—natural enough—and behold, red marks are seen on her skin. "Help, it is pulling my hair!"—some twisting and writhing, an agitated attempt to push the invisible hands away—and a consummate little actress, breathing hard, tugs her own hair down.

The Bell Spirit was an inveterate gossip. It knew everything that went on in the neighborhood, and in places far distant. We needn't take this literally, for we know how this seeming omniscience operates in the cases of spiritualist mediums and fortunetellers. One or two lucky hits and the seer's reputation is established. After that, credulous people will believe everything he says. Betsy knew the neighbors well and played with their children. Do you think children do not gossip? They are the most dangerous of gossips because they tell the literal truth. "Papa was drunk again last night; he hit Mama, and she cried, and called him . . ." Betsy listened to her friends, to the slaves—who often know a great deal more about their masters than the latter would like—and to adults, who ignore the presence of a quiet, well-behaved child. And voilà! that evening, the Spirit told all.

I won't try your patience by commenting on each

detail of this story; only think it over in the light of my suggestion, and you will find that all the pertinent facts are explained. However, I must say something about the death of John Bell, for despite my supposed prejudice against little girls I do not believe this child poisoned her father. Mr. Bell was in his late sixties. A medical man could account for his symptoms more readily than I, but I venture to suggest that any number of natural ailments, from allergies to nervous disorders, might explain his aches and pains. And Heaven knows the man had reason to suffer from nervous tension. The mysterious brown medicine that is supposed to have finished the poor gentleman off could not have produced that final coma—not if it was the same substance that sent the cat into immediate convulsions.

That Miss Betsy disliked her father I do not deny. I was struck by her remark, made some years afterward, that he often tried to prevent her from going on pleasure expeditions by lying to her. Interesting, is it not, that she should still remember this seventy years later? Mrs. Bell was happy to promote her children's pleasure; her daughter truly loved and admired this kind woman. Her stern father was only an authority symbol, and Betsy was not sorry when he died, though she would not have deliberately sought his death. Once he was gone she could enjoy herself and marry the man she secretly wanted. She was probably tired of the "witch" by that time, and was ready for more adult amusements.

• • •

"Well done, sir," the stranger said heartily. "To tell you the truth, when you gentlemen asked me to be present this evening I was a mite reluctant. I've always had a pretty dim view of this spiritualist business, and I guess I pictured you as—well—"

"Crouching over a Ouija board calling on the spirit of Aunt Sallie?" Fodor suggested with a smile.

"Something like that. I can admit it now, since I'm obliged to apologize. That was an ingenious summary, Mr. Podmore. I'm glad to see some of you gentlemen are as cynical as the members of my own profession."

"You must have known Houdini was a cynic," said Doyle, with a touch of asperity.

"I wouldn't have come if I had not known he would be here," the stranger admitted.

Even Doyle laughed at that. Houdini remarked, "You see, Sir Arthur, unlike some prophets I am not without honor in my own country. Let me add my analysis to Podmore's; as you have probably anticipated, he and I are in substantial agreement."

FIFTEEN

HOUDINI:
A CASE OF MISDIRECTION

WITH MISS BETSY in the dock and myself a member of the jury, I would have to add a second "guilty" verdict. But I wouldn't be so ungallant as to have her stand there alone. No, my friends, there would be two others with her—her brothers John and Drewry.

John admits that he and Drew were suspected of having learned "magic tricks" while in New Orleans. Now that charming old city is, and was, the home of a unique kind of black magic carried to American shores from the West Indies.

Can't you see the Bell brothers—young, healthy, curious—walking the romantic streets of New Orleans with money in their pockets and time on their hands? They wouldn't have been normal young men if they had

107

not taken advantage of the opportunity to enjoy some of the more exotic pleasures of the city. Witch doctors and conjure women, gruesome incantations and love charms—such experiences gave them tales and tricks to carry home to their unsuspecting parents and siblings.

The first raps and scratches on the outside walls of the house were produced by natural causes—wild animals, perhaps—but they stimulated the mischievous imaginations of these restless young men. Where did the first manifestations inside the house occur? Why, in the bedroom shared by the boys. And it was the younger children whose hair was pulled. Podmore has, quite rightly, mentioned the darkness in which most of these tricks occurred, but none of you city dwellers can imagine the total blackness of those country nights. It was May when Richard was lifted upright in bed by the hands clutching his hair; on a spring night, leaves and foliage would cut off even rays of moonlight, and there would be no fire to cast its dying glow.

Drewry's name keeps recurring in the earlier part of the narrative; if you remember he, as well as Betsy, "saw strange animals about the place," and it was he who violated the Indian grave and would be most likely to remember the story and his father's scolding when someone asked the Spirit to account for its presence. The next explanation the Spirit offered is even more interesting. Here, I suspect, John took a hand and set up a joke that forced his brother to put in a hard day's work digging. Drew could hardly refuse when the others were so keen without exposing his part in the plot.

Then Miss Betsy got into the act, with or without her brothers' encouragement, and the same darkness aided her performances. Think of the scene in which so many of these demonstrations took place—the Bells' reception room, in the late afternoon or at night. The windows were small, the walls thick; in that pioneer home the illumination was in all probability no more than the light of the fire.

Does that description remind you of anything, gentlemen? The conditions are exactly like the ones that prevail in most séance rooms. That is how false mediums produce their phenomena, under cover of darkness. I have exposed many of them; an ultrared photograph shows how they do it.

Now we come to the voice of the Spirit, which is certainly the most mysterious of the phenomena. Even at the time certain skeptics suspected Miss Betsy of ventriloquism, and tried to test her by placing their hands over her mouth. The Spirit spoke anyway.

Of course it did. Ventriloquism is one of the oldest of the so-called magic arts, but its mechanism was imperfectly understood at that time. There is no question of throwing the voice. The trick lies in a combination of simple breath control and misdirection—and of the two, misdirection is the more important, as it is in all sleight of hand. A trained ventriloquist learns how to muffle his tones by certain movements of tongue, lips, and throat, but even an amateur can create the impression of a distant voice simply by looking or pointing at the spot from which the voice is supposed to come. The soft whispers and whistles that passed for the Spirit's first attempts to speak are particularly hard to localize. By the time its voice reached full strength the audience believed in it, and was in a mental state of uncritical receptivity.

This is the second factor that makes for success in magic, and that contributed to the phenomenon of the Bell Spirit—the belief, if not the active collaboration, of other people. Once the existence of the Spirit was established, every unusual incident or odd coincidence was attributed to its machinations. A branch is blown from a tree during a high wind, and a boy rushes home to report that an invisible spirit is hurling missiles at him. A stray cat or dog, seen in the gray of twilight, becomes a monstrous animal. Or an amiable bachelor who has imbibed a little too much of his own excellent whiskey has a nightmare and dreams of struggling with the witch.

So the harmless joke of a pair of bored young men infected a child who was at an age ripe for mischief, and grew into a monstrous thing, nurtured by the morbid superstitions of half the county. It was beyond their control, and as their unhappy father began to suffer the normal ills of old age, exacerbated by worry and nervous hysteria, John and Drewry were unable to endure the memory of their wrongdoing. The most significant part of the case, in my opinion, is the way these men reacted to their father's death. Drewry was the only one of the Bell children who was so distressed that he became a virtual recluse, tormented by fear. Fear—or guilt? He was older than Betsy, old enough to realize his responsibility for the Frankenstein's monster he had carelessly created. He lacked the complacent conceit of John Junior, which is so evident in that gentleman's account of his dealings with the Spirit. John *had* to believe in the reality of this demon; it was his way of denying his guilt. He cursed it and condemned it, and it responded by telling him what a fine fellow he was. But it was John who threw the fatal bottle into the fire.

I don't believe in all the peculiar things you psychiatrists have invented, Fodor—your ids and your egos and your subconscious minds—but I've seen enough of human nature to know that people can actually reshape their memories of the past, forgetting the things they don't want to remember. John and Betsy succeeded in doing just that. Drewry failed, and suffered. Smile at my theory if you like, Fodor, but I'll wager that if we had been called into this case when it first began, we'd have met John and Drewry in the dark halls of the house, not Miss Betsy.

SIXTEEN

FODOR: A BUNDLE OF PROJECTED REPRESSIONS

I WOULDN'T DREAM of laughing at you, Houdini. Indeed, I must thank you for introducing a concept that forms a vital part of my own interpretation—the obliteration of unpleasant memories. The technical term for it is "repression," and I'll have more to say about it later—more, perhaps, than you wish to hear.

You made another important point when you stressed the fact that the Bell "Witch" came into existence twenty years before the birth of spiritualism. The disembodied voices and mysterious rappings of the séance room were not new. Similar demonstrations had been known for centuries, under various names. Witchcraft, haunted houses, poltergeists, psychokinesis, communica-

tion with the spirits of the dead—all are different interpretations of the same essential phenomena, reflecting
the cultural biases and backgrounds of the observers. But
the most interesting thing about the poltergeist—we may
as well continue to use that term—is that it alters its
behavior to suit the expectations of its audience. During
the Middle Ages, when witchcraft as well as knighthood
was in flower, the poltergeist performed the tricks common to witches and their familiars. After the advent of
spiritualism, the same noisy spirits played tambourines
and trombones and told eager inquirers that they came
from a region of sunlight and love.

The unhappy Bell family was caught somewhere in
the middle. Mr. Bell and his more intelligent friends
denied the possibility of witchcraft. Others were more
susceptible to the old superstition, and from these individuals we get the stories of black dogs and other strange
animals, of evil smells and horses that refuse to move—all
typical of the medieval witch's performance.

Eliminate these, however, and we are left with facts
that are all the more significant because they do not fit
into a preconceived framework. Perhaps that is why we
find them contradictory and baffling. We, too, are accustomed to see psychic phenomena conform to an uncon-
sciously accepted pattern of belief.

Yes, gentlemen, there it is—the word you have all
expected and dreaded—the unconscious! In that single
word we have the true explanation of the poltergeist. It is
not a ghost or a disembodied spirit. It is a part of the

haunted person—a segment of his or her own mind. No wonder it expresses itself in terms of the individual's cultural milieu.

I assume you are all familiar with the concept of multiple personality. It has formed the subject of a number of popular books and films. The landmark study of this phenomenon was made around the turn of the century by Dr. Morton Prince. He was consulted by a young woman named Christine Beauchamp, after a nervous breakdown had reduced her to a wreck of her former self. In the course of his analysis Dr. Prince found Christine to be an abnormally shy, withdrawn young woman, oppressed by a puritanical conscience. A conventional enough case, so far; imagine the good doctor's consternation when one day an unfamiliar voice addressed him through this girl's lips.

Christine had no less than three separate personalities. Not only did they speak in different voices, but the very appearance of the body they occupied changed. The most engaging of the three was laughing, fun-loving Sally. Christine knew nothing of this person, but Sally knew all about Christine, and despised her for her meekness and sobriety. Often she played rude practical jokes on her alter ego, taking over the communal body and going for long walks. When she submerged herself and allowed Christine to waken, the bewildered young woman found herself miles from home with no memory of how she had gotten there.

I need not point out to you the dazzling significance

of this discovery for psychic research. The spirit "controls" who speak through an entranced medium—the demon who possesses an innocent child and performs unspeakable obscenities—the poltergeist itself—may not these be examples of such a schizophrenic disturbance? Consider some of the characteristics of these secondary personalities, as reported by analysts who have studied them, and see how well they conform to the characteristics of the poltergeist.

Because the secondary personality is a rejected and suppressed segment of the mind, it is the direct antithesis of the original personality—cheerful and frivolous instead of serious, vulgar instead of puritanical, free and easy instead of shy. Often its behavior verges on the infantile; it plays practical jokes and makes rude remarks, as a child would do.

The secondary personality is extremely susceptible to suggestion. It may even be brought into existence by the indirect, unconscious hints of the therapist. Furthermore, it often displays greater intelligence than the original personality. Some spirit "controls" have written poetry and even complete books, have composed music and invented entire new languages. The explanation for this lies in the fact—I will try to put it as simply as possible—that the brain is a vast storehouse of untapped information. Somewhere in that mysterious labyrinth lies every scrap of information ever received, heard, or read. The unconscious mind can refer to memories, detailed and vivid, which the conscious mind has utterly forgotten.

The Bell Spirit was such a secondary personality. Its infantile behavior, its uncanny familiarity with Scripture and religious literature, its vulgar expressions—all fit the diagnosis of schizophrenic dissociation familiar to psychoanalysts. It did not develop into full and active existence until the unwitting Mr. Johnson challenged it to respond to his questions, and from that time on it reacted precisely as the individuals who encountered it expected it to react—singing hymns to Mrs. Bell, cursing and threatening the slaves, debating theology with the preacher.

So far so good, Podmore and Houdini will say. My theory is a little farfetched, but it accords with their belief that Betsy Bell's hands and vocal cords produced the tricks that came to be called the Bell Witch. Not at all, gentlemen.

The agent was not Betsy, but Betsy II—a split-off part of the girl's mind, functioning without her conscious knowledge. And it did not always employ Betsy's physical body.

I agree with Podmore that fraud is responsible for many poltergeist cases. But not all—no, not all. The disturbed personality demonstrates a form of energy. Children approaching puberty are almost by definition disturbed; they displace enormous amounts of psychic energy. Recent studies in extrasensory perception have proved beyond a doubt that such mental powers exist. The most significant of them, from our point of view, is psychokinesis—PK, as it is sometimes called—the ability to move objects by purely mental energy. Experiments at Duke University in America, at Freiburg in Germany, and more recently in the Soviet Union indicate that even under laboratory conditions certain individuals can produce and control this force. When it is the product of strong emotion or mental disturbance, the force is even more powerful. There was undoubtedly some fraud in the Bell case, but I do not doubt that Betsy II, the dissociated, disembodied fragment of the girl's mind, was able to affect and modify physical space by means of psychic energy.

Such disturbances are not produced by casual neuroses, they are the result of a profound cleavage, an explosive loosening of an infantile part of the psyche in which severe conflicts are repressed. What could cause this psychic lobotomy in a healthy young girl?

The Spirit hated John Bell. If it was indeed a part of Betsy Bell's mind, the conclusion is inescapable. Betsy hated her father. Her conscious mind had to suppress her hatred and the guilt it induced. This bundle of repressions was projected in the form of a poltergeist, who tried to work out the conflict by expressing both emotions in action—destruction of the hated parent and self-punishment for the crime. John Bell died; Betsy Bell was tormented and deprived of her lover.

But why did Betsy hate her father? Dislike is not hate, normal childish resentment of a stern parent is not a sufficient motive for murder. The onset of puberty in Betsy was the catalyst that gave birth to the Spirit. This event is often linked with outbursts of poltergeist activity. Why not? It is an event of great emotional and physical upheaval. The onset of puberty in the female is marked by a dramatic physical change, with terrifying psychological implications. In earlier times the cultural-societal implications were equally traumatic. From the strictures of St. Paul to the medical opinions of nineteenth-century physicians, women were taught that they were vessels of iniquity; that no pure woman desired or enjoyed sexual intercourse; that their natural feelings and needs were sinful. It is a wonder, my friends, that any woman ever made a reasonable adjustment to this preposterous concept. It is no wonder that some of them found the adjustment impossible. Podmore's investigations indicated, correctly, that in the past the majority of poltergeist frauds were naughty little girls. The picture has changed in recent years, as outmoded sexual conventions have given way to a healthier attitude. We now find as many, or more, naughty little boys!

In Betsy Bell's case, however, some more intense trauma must have caused the intense hatred of her father and the resulting dissociation. My suggestion is purely speculative. It will shock and appall some of you. But it is based on years of clinical experience in psychology.

John Bell took sexual liberties with his daughter. This is the worst traumatic foundation for the development of later psychosis or neurosis.

John Bell's physical symptoms were self-induced, by shame and guilt. They are classic examples of psychosomatic disorders. The swelling of his tongue and the pain in his jaws, which prevented him from speaking—from confessing his sin; the nervous tics and convulsions, signs of irrepressible conflict and self-punishment. Child molestation, gentlemen, is not confined to brutish, uneducated men. It has occurred in the best families and in men of outwardly puritanical habits. Betsy, too young to fully comprehend what had been done to her, repressed her horror until the shock of puberty produced a regressive earthquake. If a fragment of her personality had not split off under the unbearable strain, she would probably have ended up in a hospital for the insane. Therapeutically the "witch" saved her reason. By revenging herself on her father, and punishing herself by self-mutilation and the loss of her lover, she attained sanity and lived, as we have seen, to a ripe and healthy old age.

But I see Sir Arthur is about to burst with indignation. Speak, my friend. I am ready for your criticism and your reproaches.

SEVENTEEN

DOYLE:
A VOICE FROM BEYOND

I DON'T KNOW which appalls me more, Fodor—your
dreadful suggestion, or the mind that could conceive
such a thing. But I suppose you can't help it; you fellows
who spend your lives prying into people's innermost
thoughts are bound to have a distorted view of the world.
I know you mean well, and I don't condemn you.

But I do reproach you—all of you—for the cavalier
manner in which you blandly throw out any evidence
that does not agree with your prejudices. "Discard this,
ignore that, we need not take such tales seriously . . ." If
you can't fit a document into a pigeonhole, you throw it
into a wastebasket.

Your bundle of projected repressions, my learned
friend, is a bundle of nonsense. Why, if everyone who

suffered from suppressed emotions projected them in such a form, half the houses in the country would be afflicted with poltergeists. Your schizophrenia doesn't fit, either. You yourself said that the original personality is usually shy and puritanical. Betsy was cheerful, healthy, outgoing—the exact opposite of Miss Beauchamp, and "Eve" and the other cases we've read about.

As for the suggestion of conscious fraud made by Houdini and Podmore—yes, many mediums and child poltergeists have been caught playing tricks. I admit that, but I believe they only resort to fraud when their spiritual powers fail for one reason or another. You investigators observe a youngster playing a trick and then conclude that all the phenomena, even the ones you didn't see, were produced by trickery. If that's your idea of logic, I want no part of it.

You are only correct about one thing. Betsy Bell was the center of the disturbances. Why, gentlemen, isn't it obvious that Betsy was a powerful natural medium? This is proved beyond the shadow of a doubt by her convulsive seizures. I have seen the same thing happen when a spiritual entity attempted to gain control of the body of an inexperienced medium. A trained sensitive can help a discarnate entity to accomplish this without difficulty. The "control" can then speak through the medium; having no vocal cords of his own, he has no other means of achieving the direct communication such spirits desperately desire. Betsy was unfamiliar with the procedure; it frightened her so badly that she resisted instead of helping, and after seeing that it was causing the girl pain and distress, the Spirit considerately refrained from its attempts.

There is evidence that when a life has been cut short before it has reached the term God set for it, a residue of psychic force remains, which has to work itself out. Such was the origin of the Bell Spirit. As soon as someone had the courage and the intelligence to question it, it replied.

If only the admirable Mr. Johnson and the good ministers of the gospel had had more experience! They did their best, but they did not know how to guide a troubled spirit to its rest.

The first, spontaneous reply of the Spirit to the question "Who are you and why are you here?" holds the key to the mystery—a key which, tragically, was never used. "I was once happy, but have been made to suffer and am now unhappy." How often have I heard similar statements! How often have I had the happiness of assisting a disembodied sufferer to understand its conditions or to fulfill an unfinished task, before guiding it into the beautiful world awaiting it.

Very often, too, I have heard frivolous and mischievous replies such as the ones that misled the earnest questioners of the Bell Spirit. For once contact has been made, once the door to the other world has been set ajar, a host of waiting intelligences may crowd through. This well-known fact accounts for the seeming contradictions of the Spirit's behavior. There was not one single Spirit, there were many. One, the dominant, original visitor, was the sweet-voiced singer of hymns who quoted Scripture with such touching effect and who loved the goodness of Mrs. Lucy Bell. Others, such as the "witch family," are clearly examples of mischievous spirits, and I don't know why you should be surprised that disembodied spirits should be hoaxers. The same intelligence, inside a human body, often derives amusement from capricious tricks. The silly man, the arrogant man, the cocksure man is always a safe butt for such a joker.

The phenomena that have driven you gentlemen to such questionable lengths in attempting to explain them are commonplace to psychic investigators. Materialization of objects such as the fruit offered Mrs. Bell, the sensitivity of animals to spiritual presences, the ability of a discarnate entity to conquer the limitations of space and time—such things have been observed and recorded, not once but many times. None of the features of this case is unique, not even the voice. Mrs. Crandon, the marvelous medium to whom Houdini here was so unkind, had a control named Harry, whose voice and vocabulary were decidedly masculine, quite unlike her own refined tones. And you, Fodor, investigated the "talking mongoose" case in 1931; you granted the similarities between its voice and that of the Bell Spirit, and admitted you did not believe the mystery would ever be solved.

I have no doubt that a strong strain of mediumistic sensitivity ran in the Bell family, inherited, no doubt, from Mrs. Bell. Once aroused this continued to function, and displayed itself in its highest form in John Bell Junior. This man was no ignorant farmer, he was an officer and a magistrate. His son was a physician, his grandson a specialist in mental disorders and a trained scientist. Houdini's sneers at these witnesses display his prejudice, as does his suggestion that Dr. Charles was suffering from senility when he wrote his book. Sixty-four, my friends, is not so great an age as that.

In the communications given to John Bell Junior the Spirit demonstrated the highest qualities. I have no doubt that the entity of 1828 was the first visitor, now wiser and more advanced in the spiritual realm. The jeering tricksters did not intrude, in part because the Spirit was in firmer control and in part because John Junior was more competent than his young sister. You complain of the vague predictions made by this Spirit; I do not see how predictions can be more precise. The War Between the States, the first Great War and the portents of the second—all were mentioned and described.

Gentlemen, you have been quick to accuse the dead, who are mute and defenseless and cannot speak for themselves. How can you be so complacent? However much our tiny human brains may try to classify such extraordinary matters, there still remain so many unknown causes and unexplained conditions that our best efforts can only be regarded as well-meant approximations to the truth.

• • •

Conan Doyle's voice trembled with emotion. After a moment Fodor said quietly, "You do well to remind us of our limitations, Sir Arthur. It is only a game we play tonight; none of us would have the effrontery to pretend we have offered the ultimate solution. But we have yet to hear from our guest. Inspector Ryan, you are a practical man, with years of experience in a large city police department. What is your solution?"

"I don't want to offend Sir Arthur," the guest began. "But if he were to consider the case as Mr. Sherlock Holmes might have done—"

"You will never win his support by referring to that personage," Houdini said dryly. "He tried to murder him, you know."

"And I only regret that I failed." Doyle's eyes twinkled. "Never mind my feelings, Inspector, my curiosity is as keen as anyone's. Which of our interpretations do you prefer?"

"Why, sir," said Ryan calmly, "none, sir. None of you has come near the truth."

EIGHTEEN

INSPECTOR RYAN:
MALICE DOMESTIC

F irst I want to thank you for inviting me here
tonight, gentlemen. You have sure given me a lot of
new ideas. I hope I can return the favor. Frankly, I am
amazed none of you has seen what is, in my humble opinion, the most significant aspect of this unusual case.

It is a case of murder.

Sir Arthur hit the nail on the head when he said you
all throw out the facts that don't fit your theory. Dr.
Fodor is the only one of you who has come to grips with
John Bell's death, and he hasn't considered the evidence.
Why, gentlemen, no responsible physician would sign
the death certificate of a man who died under such circumstances. John Bell was not a young man, but he was
in excellent health till the trouble began; some of his

contemporaries lived to be over ninety. John Bell was deliberately done to death—poisoned—and there is only one person who could have killed him. That person wasn't Miss Betsy. That person was his wife.

One rule of police theory is that in cases of domestic murder the primary suspect is always the husband or wife. So I started my mental investigation with Mrs. Bell. But I admit I was dumbfounded when I realized that every single bit of evidence pointed straight to her. She is not only the principal suspect, she is the only person who could have committed the crime.

John Bell was gravely ill but still conscious on December eighteenth. On the morning of the nineteenth his son found him in a deep coma from which he never awoke. Clearly the murderous potion was administered to him on the night of the eighteenth. And who was with him the whole night? Why, Mrs. Bell. Did you note that revealing sentence in her son's narrative—"Mother slipped away from the bedside where she had sat all night long"? Even without that I would have assumed Mrs. Bell had been with her husband; where else would a devoted wife be when her husband lay mortally ill?

This fact in itself is almost enough to condemn Mrs. Bell. There is one other suspect. By his own statement, John Junior was in charge of his father's medicine. He could have given Mr. Bell the fatal dose without comment or suspicion from his mother. But John Junior could not have committed the other acts that led up to the murder.

Mrs. Bell must have been poisoning her husband for several years. The numbness and swelling of his tongue suggest some kind of vegetable poison, administered by mouth. Mrs. Bell isn't the only person who could have slipped a pinch of poison into his hot toddy or his glass of whiskey, but the individual who had constant access to what he ate and drank was his wife, the supervisor of the kitchen.

So much for opportunity. Let us now consider the means by which Mrs. Bell might have obtained poison.

The fields and forests of our beautiful country contain enough poisonous substances to wipe out half the population. The pretty foxglove, the common pokeberry—the berries of a dozen different shrubs—why, gentlemen, nature is a poisoner! In that pioneer society the lady of the house had to be an amateur doctor; she took care of her family and servants in cases of minor illness. If her medicine chest didn't hold what she needed to kill her husband, she could gather a few leaves and brew up gallons of noxious liquids without anyone asking what she was doing. Finding that the old gentleman was too tough to succumb to the first concoction, she got impatient and tried something else. John Bell's deep coma could have resulted from an overdose of a narcotic, such as opium. Laudanum—a mixture of opium and alcohol—was part of every housewife's pharmacopoeia in the nineteenth century. The cat's reaction to the mysterious liquid is susceptible to several explanations. Maybe the bottle John found wasn't the laudanum, but one of Mrs. Bell's other brews. The cat's convulsions sound like the same tetanic seizures John Bell suffered in the last few months of his life. His wife may have tried a dozen different substances before one finally finished him.

Why would a good, virtuous lady like that want to kill her good, virtuous husband? I ask you, gentlemen—who knows the hidden angers and secret resentments felt by married people? But I know one thing—if Mrs. Bell wanted to be free of Mr. Bell, murder was the only way out for a woman of her temperament and station in life. And it was beginning to look as if the old man would live forever. I can't talk about motive, it is buried in the grave. I don't need to. The other facts are damning enough. Mrs. Bell had the best opportunity to kill her husband, and she is the only one who could have created the Spirit.

Take almost every one of the weird tricks it performed, including some of those you've eliminated as too preposterous to be true, and you'll find that Mrs. Bell could have done them. The voice of the Spirit, for instance. You talk about misdirection—it never occurred to anyone to suspect the pious housewife. She could howl like a banshee and the audience wouldn't even look in her direction. The believers would exclaim in wonder and the skeptics would be watching Betsy.

Mrs. Bell could be out of her bed all night long, and if anybody caught her wandering around she had a dozen excuses. She forgot to put the milk away, or she thought she heard one of the kiddies crying . . . Her hard-working husband probably slept like the dead—even assuming he hadn't been drugged by his loving spouse. As soon as he was snoring off went Lucy, tip-toeing into the children's rooms to scratch and slap, visiting the neighbors to eavesdrop on their private conversations. When Mrs. Bell was sick, the Spirit shut its mouth while she was sleeping. It started to talk when she woke up.

Remember the sermons that were quoted so accurately? That was a cute trick, and I'm surprised Mr. Houdini hasn't spotted how it could have been worked. Mrs. Bell had undoubtedly heard one of the sermons. She was a regular churchgoer. She had heard the other preacher, too, dozens of times, she was acquainted with his style of talking, and one of her friends might have mentioned the subject of his sermon that Sunday—even given her a synopsis of the talk. Why, that was what they discussed at those Sunday night prayer meetings, wasn't it? She wouldn't have had to repeat the sermons word for word; a reasonably accurate imitation would have been accepted as miraculous by her superstitious audience.

And take the decision to send for the witch doctor, a decision known only to Mr. Bell and the two messengers. At first the "all-knowing" Spirit was baffled by this, but by evening it had learned the truth. Now, gentlemen, wouldn't Mr. Bell finally yield to the pleas of his wife and confide in her? Ladies have a lot of little tricks for wheedling information out of their husbands. The "phantom" hand held for an instant by Calvin Johnson was a woman's hand. The voices were all female, even those of the four members of the witch family.

Mrs. Bell created the Spirit, but it wasn't long before other people took a hand. Miss Betsy, and perhaps some of the others, played tricks on their own account. There's your naughty little girl, Mr. Podmore. She became the center of attention—the sweet child martyr. Few kiddies could resist that role. Besides, it must have been useful for getting her out of chores she didn't want to do. You can't ask a girl who has been beaten by a witch to wash the dishes.

From the start the Spirit doted on Mrs. Bell. "Luce, poor Luce—the best woman alive." That's a dead give-away right there. As for the way the others were treated, the only one who really suffered was the husband. The children didn't get anything worse than the tweaks and smacks any exasperated parent may be moved to bestow on them. It isn't unusual for a mother to prefer her sons— or one particular son—to her daughters, and fathers often spoil their little girls. I don't buy your notion that Mr. Bell molested his daughter, Doctor—not because it shocks me, the Good Lord knows I've encountered too many such cases—but because there's no evidence to support it. Mr. Bell could have been innocently fond of his pretty golden-haired daughter, and his wife could have been jealous. But I think it's more likely that Betsy pulled her own hair and fell into fake fits to get attention.

Dr. Fodor, I don't hold with your idea that sex is at the bottom of everything, but your talk about split personalities gave me some new insights. I've heard about such cases, but don't you see that the things you said about little Betsy apply even more neatly to her mother? Here's a lady at a certain time of life, a lady known for her piety and kindness. By George, she must have had a good-sized bundle of repressions built up. I guess Dr. Fodor would say Mrs. Bell's repressed hostility and frustration split off into a separate personality—a Mrs. Hyde, so to speak. That would explain why the Spirit's first remarks were so pious and mealy-mouthed. It was testing, making sure its little game was going to work. Once it was accepted as an outside agent, it could let itself go and say all the nasty things Mrs. Bell had never allowed herself to say. I'm told that some of the most delicate, refined ladies cut loose with language that would make a muleskinner blush when they are under anaesthesia. They know the words. Mrs. Bell knew them too, just as she knew a lot of neighborhood gossip she wouldn't repeat when she was herself.

The conclusive piece of evidence is the second visit of the Spirit. Betsy is cleared by that, if by nothing else; she wasn't even living at home in 1828. Neither was John Junior. But his house wasn't far away; did his mother take long walks on those spring evenings, or were the conversations about future wars and the martyrdom of our Saviour the product of John Junior's restless imagination? It doesn't matter. Mrs. Bell was living in the old homestead when the rappings returned for the second time. By 1935, when the Spirit was due to return for its third visit, she had been in her grave for almost a century. Poor woman! Once I might have called her something else, but I've learned a thing or two tonight. I believe it was not Mrs. Bell but Mrs. Hyde—Lucy II, as Dr. Fodor would call her—who committed the murder. God knows what drove her to it. May she rest in peace.

Houdini struck his hands together. His gray eyes shone.

"I like it. I like it! Inspector, you put us to shame. I think you've got it."

Fodor stroked his chin. "A most convincing argument."

"Horrible," Doyle cried. "Unjust and unfair. I don't believe it for a moment."

"Neither do I," Podmore said. "Your arguments are ingenious, Inspector. But my explanation also covers all the facts, and child poltergeists are the common rule. Miss Betsy fits the pattern too well."

"Your child poltergeist is only one of the possible patterns," Fodor objected. "Of all the theories put forth this evening—"

NINETEEN

SUMMERS: PLAYING WITH HELL FIRE

"ALL ARE most damnably in error."

The deep sepulchral voice seemed to issue from the empty air. Even the imperturbable Podmore started. Doyle glared wildly around the room, as if he feared that the Bell Spirit had returned to make its comment on the proceedings.

A high-backed leather chair stood slightly to one side of the circle in which the friends were sitting. With unnerving abruptness a face rose into view over the back of the chair—a round, rosy, smiling face whose generous chin was supported by a clerical collar. This apparition went on, its tone and its language quite at variance with its benevolent appearance.

"Your ignoble fatuities and monstrous extrava-

gances, gentlemen, indicate that you are totally ignorant of the subject. The true nature of the Bell Witch is
hideously apparent to anyone with an open mind. This
suffering child, this unhappy maiden, was doomed to
suffer because of the ignoble heresies of Calvin and
Knox. The misguided ministers had neither the spiritual nor the practical knowledge to deal with so dark
and difficult a task. The only thing that could have
saved Betsy Bell was an exorcist—*spiritualis
imperator*—specifically ordained to cast out demons by
the grace of the Holy Ghost.

"Yes! This was a clear and dreadful case of diabolic
possession. Have we not the authority of God's holy
word as to its reality? 'Behold, they brought him a dumb
man possessed with a devil, and after the devil was cast
out, the dumb man spoke.' (Matthew nine, gentlemen—verses thirty-two and thirty-three.)

"History records innumerable examples of obses-
sion and diabolic possession. That unhappy home in
Tennessee saw another. At first the demon attacked the
Bell family from without, by knocks and rappings and
physical attacks. This is technically known as obses-
sion. It is often the prelude to actual possession, in
which the demon assumes control of an individual's
body from within. Betsy Bell's seizures, or fainting fits,
were unmistakable signs of possession. The filthy
obscenities voiced by the creature, its knowledge of all
languages, the foul stench noted by one witness—all
are signs of the presence of an unclean spirit. Or, in this

case, spirits. Scripture tells us that a demonic presence admitted its name was Legion—innumerable, countless. With what typical frivolity did you dismiss one of the most important clues in the narrative—the witch family, and the devilishly significant name of its leader. A black dog was one of the commonest manifestations of that oldest and most vile of fallen angels.

"Sir Arthur, you appear flushed. No wonder! Don't you realize you are playing with fire—Hell fire—when you summon the dead? The voices you hear at your séances are not dear ones who have passed from this life, they are demonic actors of diabolic skill. The New Religion of Spiritualism is but the Old Witchcraft, and the Bell Witch was indeed a witch—a vile, perverse, and perverting spirit like the ones that led the Salem witches to death and damnation. Spiritualism is most foul, most loathly, most—"

Doyle surged to his feet. "By Heaven, Summers, you go too far! This was a private conversation which—"

"Which was on the verge of concluding," Houdini interrupted, taking his irate friend firmly by the arm. "Shall we go, gentlemen?"

"We may as well." Podmore shot a glance of cold dislike at the disembodied head, which grinned back at him. "There is no hope of intelligent discussion now. Good night, Mr. Summers."

"Reverend Summers, sir! And let me warn you, Sir Arthur—"

Doyle's friends surrounded him and led him out. In

the hall, while they waited for the servant to fetch their coats, the Inspector asked incredulously, "Who the devil is that madman?"

"He is no priest, whatever he pretends," Doyle sputtered.

"His name is Montague Summers," Fodor explained. "He is the author of a number of learned books on magic and witchcraft which are distinguished by the astonishing fact that the man believes in each and all of these superstitions. He deplores the fact that the witch finders were not thorough enough, and considers burning to death too light a punishment for persons who have embraced Satanism."

"You're kidding," Ryan said. "Or is he?"

"No, he is quite in earnest. Strangely enough," Fodor said thoughtfully, "he has done quite a nice job of editing the major Restoration dramatists."

"Oh, what does it matter?" Houdini slipped into his overcoat and took his hat from the cloakroom attendant. "The fellow is a bad joke. If Sir Arthur hadn't been on the verge of losing his temper, I'd have encouraged Summers to rave on. He is funnier than a vaudeville show."

The front door opened; a gray tendril of fog slid in, like a ghostly arm. Podmore turned up his collar. Fodor contemplated the spectral glow of a street lamp, eerily swathed in mist.

"We part here, gentlemen," he said. "A strange conclusion to our evening. We had dispelled the ghosts and demons, only to have them raised again by Summers."

"Perhaps it was a fitting conclusion after all," Houdini said musingly. "Our theories offer satisfying explanations, but in spite of all our logic we will never know the true answer—unless in some other universe we are privileged to meet Mrs. Betsy Bell Powell face-to-face, and hear the story from her own lips. We might not care for that, you know. It would be a dull world if all doubts were resolved and all questions answered—a world without wonder or scope for imagination . . ."

The five men part. Their forms melt into the fog and disappear.

The Second Evening

TWENTY

"**T**HE FOG THICKENS," said Conan Doyle in solemn tones.

He stood at the tall window, which was framed by heavy red plush draperies. Outside, the wrought-iron railings glistened with condensed moisture. All objects beyond them were wrapped in a veil of fog; the forms of passersby moved like shrouded spectres, and the gas lamps shone with a ghostly glow.

His companion laughed. "An appropriate setting, isn't it? Like the start of one of your famous stories. Come and sit down, Arthur, and let the servant draw the curtains."

With the dreary night shut out the room felt cozy and comfortable. A fire crackled on the hearth and handsome oriental rugs muffled the footsteps of the servants moving about the room. Several overstuffed chairs had been drawn up in a semicircle facing the fire. Instead of taking one of them, Doyle turned, courteously awaiting the arrival of the others. They were not long in following: thin-faced, intense Frank Podmore, who had been called the skeptic-in-chief of the Society for Psychical Research; the suave Viennese psychiatrist, Nandor Fodor; and, preceding them, the sole American member of their informal society, gallantly excorting a lady whose hand rested lightly on his arm. Harry Houdini was not a tall man, but the lady's crown of thick auburn hair barely reached his ear. Like the men, she wore formal evening attire; the skirts of her satin gown trailed behind her and the bodice glittered with jet and crystal beads. She was not in her first youth, but Doyle, a gentleman of the old school, had privately decided she was still a fine figure of a woman. He was too much of a gentleman to wonder whether the color of her hair was entirely natural.

The lady examined the pleasant room and its elegant furnishings with interest. "Well, this is a privilege," she remarked, her deep contralto voice marked (not unpleasantly, Doyle thought) by an unmistakable American accent. "I never expected to be admitted to such a bastion of masculine privacy. How did you get me in?"

Houdini chuckled, and led her to a chair in the center of the circle. "The rules of that other world—I won't

call it the real world, since this one suits me just fine—
are suspended here, ma'am. If this were a traditional
gentleman's club, I probably wouldn't have been admitted either!"

Andrew Lang, who had already seated himself, rose
politely, and the others waited until she had taken a
chair before selecting their own. Brandy and coffee were
ordered. Houdini lit a cigar, and Fodor took out his
pipe. The lady fumbled in her unfashionably large
evening bag and produced a packet of cigarettes. She
was still rummaging around in it, presumably for a
means of lighting her cigarette, when Harry Price, on
her right, struck a match for her.

She acknowledged the gesture with a smile. "I'm
honored all the same, gentlemen, to be part of such a distinguished company as this! You are all authorities on the
subject of the occult, and I am the merest amateur."

A courteous murmur of denial followed the statement, and the lady smiled more broadly. "In fact, I have
drawn extensively from your works for my own humble
literary efforts. Yet I venture to suggest that we writers
of fiction may occasionally contribute a kind of insight
that eludes the strictly rational mind."

She nodded at Doyle, who beamed back at her.
"Exactly," he said eagerly. "The creative impulse—"

He broke off to take a glass from the tray the waiter
offered. The lady had refused brandy, and Doyle said
with anxious courtesy, "Would you prefer another beverage, ma'am?"

The lady coughed deprecatingly. "Since you are kind enough to ask, Sir Arthur, a whiskey and soda would be just the thing. I hope that doesn't shock you."

Houdini laughed and beckoned the waiter. "An excellent idea, ma'am. I'll join you."

Fodor, pipe in hand, leaned forward. "What you were saying of the creative impulse is of course correct. Whence such inspirations come is unknown, but that they may tap a source of knowledge hidden from the common mind is unquestionable."

"Are you implying that mine is a common mind?" Price asked. His well-schooled countenance remained grave, but there was a twinkle in his eyes. Fodor, who knew him well, smiled and replied, "Not common, Price, but certainly limited! As is mine. I bow to the talents of our writers of fiction, including Andrew, of course."

Lang shook his head. "My little fairy tales aren't my own creations, you know. Like our charming guest, I am an amateur on the subject of folklore and the supernatural; but, like her, I have read widely and given the matter much thought. I look forward to her exposition with interest. Am I correct in assuming that we are to have another American ghost story this evening?"

"Quite," said the lady. After an appreciative sip of her whiskey, she put the glass down on the table, extinguished her cigarette, and dug into her bag with both hands. They emerged with a sheaf of paper, which she displayed triumphantly. "The Phelps case. We Americans do seem to specialize in poltergeists, don't we, Mr. Houdini?"

"People call them that," said Houdini cynically. "Most of it's trickery and sleight of hand."

Conan Doyle snorted vigorously, and Price remarked, "Never mind, Sir Arthur. We know your views. It is the disagreement among our views that produces such interesting discussions during these informal meetings. As for poltergeists, they are not a purely American phenomenon. I've investigated dozens of such cases in England."

"But you can't investigate this one," said Lang. "Except by inference." He went on, addressing their visitor. "We restrict ourselves, ma'am, to cases that have never been properly investigated or explained—the classic unsolved mysteries of the occult."

"So I have been given to understand," said the lady. "The case I have selected is certainly one of the most famous of those mysteries, at least to those of us who are familiar with the literature of the occult. I have written it in the guise of fiction, but I believe you will find that the basic facts are all there."

Removing a pair of horn-rimmed spectacles from her bag, she set them on her nose, took another sip of whiskey, cleared her throat genteelly, and began reading.

TWENTY-ONE

W<small>E DO NOT</small> have all the facts. We have
only fragmentary reports, distorted by the
prejudices of the observers. The journalists of mid-
nineteenth-century America did not intrude into the
private lives of respectable people. Dr. Eliakim Phelps
was a man of the cloth, his wife a lady of good family.
Once the bizarre business had ended, they retreated
into the obscurity they desired and deserved.

Had he but known, the Reverend Dr. Phelps was
lucky he lived when he did. One hundred and fifty years
later television crews would have surrounded the house,
hoping for footage of ghosts and children possessed by
devils; the servants would have appeared on talk shows,
and the speculations of the neighbors would have

appeared in print and on the evening news broadcasts. Would the truth have emerged from this flood of information and misinformation? Perhaps not. We will probably never know for certain what eerie force invaded the quiet parsonage in Stratford, Connecticut, in the year 1850. But this is how it might have happened . . .

TWENTY-TWO

WHEN I FIRST set eyes on Stratford, I thought it was such a quiet, peaceful little town. Now I hate it. What have we done to bring this horror upon us? The ladies still speak to me when I meet them in the shops or on the street; they can hardly fail to do so, when my husband is their clergyman. But they cluster in little murmuring groups after I pass; the buzzing grumble of their gossip follows me like a swarm of angry bees. I do not turn or look back, but sometimes I long to whirl and shout at them, "Say it—say it to my face! Give me a chance to answer back, instead of whispering lies."

They say our invisible tormentors are devils, damned souls sent to punish us for some hidden sin. Andrew (he said I might call him Andrew) insists they are spirits of good. I wish I could be sure. When he spoke, when I was in his presence, I believed him. He has such a wonderful voice. His fiery dark eyes, his handsome features, his tall, youthful frame—his entire being vibrates with such sincerity that I am carried away by it. But he has gone now—never to return? I walk out to do my marketing or take a little exercise—and the whispers buzz behind me. I wish I were back in Philadelphia. I wish I had never married. But what else could I have done? I was alone—grieving for my deceased husband, helpless as women always are without a strong man to lean on, my children suffering from the lack of a father's care.

I have never been, nor wanted to be, a disciplinarian. I am sure children respond more readily to affection. After their dear papa passed on I did not have the heart to punish the children for trivial acts of mischief. They missed their father—Henry particularly. He is such a sensitive boy.

When the Reverend Dr. Phelps proposed marriage to me, my answer was, in some degree, influenced by the needs of my children But not entirely—oh, no. Mr. Phelps is a fine man. Fine-looking, too, for his age—not that sixty is old . . . He seems older because he is so serious and scholarly. I respect him very much.

When I told him I would be his wife he kissed me gently on the brow. Then he took his leave, promising to return that evening to greet the children as their new papa.

After he had gone I stood in the downstairs hall, looking up the stairs. The weather was dreary, dark and chill; snow hissed against the windows like whispering voices. I was conscious of a strange and inexplicable reluctance to ascend those stairs. As I hesitated, my hand on the knob of the newel post, it seemed to me that there was something up there, just out of sight around the turn of the stairs. A dark, shapeless shadow loomed on the wall of the landing.

I know now that it was a portent, a foreshadowing of what was to come. It could have been nothing else. No danger awaited me at the top of the stairs, only the nursery and my darling children. The two little ones would be tucked in their cribs now, but I had promised to come to Harry after Mr. Phelps left.

The shadow was gone. It had never really been there; I knew that. But my feet dragged as I mounted the stairs.

After the gloom of the hallway the nursery looked bright and cheerful. A fire crackled on the hearth. I reminded myself not to call it "the nursery." Harry disliked the word. He was too old, he insisted, for a nurse or a nursery. Soon he would be all of twelve years old!

He sat on the rug before the fire, his legs crossed and his chin propped on his hands. He was playing with his little toy theatre, his favorite plaything of all the toys I had given him. It was an elaborate affair, though it was made of pasteboard and the characters were cut out of paper. It had real red satin curtains and a small stage. Harry often put on performances for me, taking all the parts himself and moving his paper people around the stage as he spoke in voices that moved from gruff to falsetto. *Hamlet* and *Julius Caesar* were among his favorites—in greatly abridged versions, of course. Apparently some new play was being plotted, for there were only two cardboard personages on the stage—a slender, ringletted female who usually represented the heroine, and a villainous-looking person who had been Cassius and Hamlet's wicked uncle in his time.

TWENTY-THREE

HARRY LOOKED UP. His face brightened when he saw me, and he brushed a lock of unruly brown hair from his eyes.

"Mama," he cried, jumping up and running to embrace me. "You were so long!"

I put my arms around his sturdy shoulders, noting, with half a smile and half a sigh, how tall and stout he was growing. He would not be "Mama's dear little boy" much longer. I had encouraged him to consider himself "the man of the family."

"I am sorry, my darling. Mr. Phelps has just this moment left."

"Why does he come so often and stay so long?" Harry demanded. "I wish he would not come."

"Harry, you mustn't say such things," came a quiet voice from the corner of the room. It was Marian, my daughter. Marian always sits in corners and speaks in a quiet voice. It is easy to forget that Marian is in the room. She is plain and her disposition is not engaging, but she has a good heart. Her devotion to her brother is the finest part of her character.

"Never mind, Marian," I said. "Harry only means that he misses his mama. I miss you too, Harry. But I hope you will be polite to Mr. Phelps. You will see more of him . . . I mean to say . . . You don't really dislike him, do you, darling? He is a good man—"

"I hate him!" Harry stepped back. Fists clenched, face crimson, he looked challengingly at me.

Marian rose, putting down the book she had been reading. "He doesn't mean it, Mama. Don't be upset. He only says it to vex you."

"Why, Marian, how spiteful you are," I exclaimed. "Harry would never wish to vex me."

"Never, Mama." My son flung his arms around me. "I love you, Mama."

"And I love you, my dearest."

"So you will tell that horrid old man to go away and leave us alone?"

"Darling, he is not old or horrid."

Harry clung to me, his face hidden in my skirts. Marian said, in a flat, expressionless voice, "Are you going to marry Mr. Phelps, Mama?"

I had come to tell them that very news. I do not know

why the question rang in my ears like an accusation or a threat. I don't know why it took so long to answer.

When I said, "Yes, I am," I had my explanation all prepared. Their need of a father's love, my need of a husband's care. I had actually started my speech before I realized there was no need for it. In the same strange voice Marian murmured, "I wish you happiness, Mama."

Harry said nothing. He moved away from me. Dropping to the floor before his little theatre, he began moving the figures around the stage. His face was absorbed. The villain moved toward the maiden and pushed her over onto her cardboard back. Harry laughed in his boyish fashion.

There, I said to myself. *You see how it is—there was no need to worry. He has taken it well.*

TWENTY-FOUR

So much for the rumor put about by malicious persons that my children refused to accept their new papa. Harry's single outburst was only natural, as was Marian's calm acceptance. Marian does not feel deeply. Much as I hate to say it of a child of mine, she is rather shallow. The younger children were only six and three, too young to care for anything beyond their own little world. But Harry and I had always been close.

Certainly he did not fail in courtesy to Dr. Phelps after that, and I am frank to admit that some of the credit for their good relationship must go to Dr. Phelps himself. He treated my children as though they were his own. Well, not quite; after all, his children are fully grown, with families of their own.

Before we were married he informed me we would not be living in Philadelphia, as I had assumed. He had accepted a position as pastor of the Presbyterian church in a small town in Connecticut. Knowing what I know now, I marvel that a shudder did not pass through my body when I heard the name Stratford. But at the time—despite what some people have said—I was not reluctant to make the move. I had always loved Philadelphia, but the death of my first husband had cast a gloom over the city where we had lived together; I saw little of our former friends. Besides, it is a wife's duty to follow cheerfully and uncomplainingly wherever her husband leads.

Dr. Phelps kindly explained the reasons for his decision. His duties as pastor of the congregation in Huntington, New York, combined with his position as secretary of the Presbyterian Educational Society in Philadelphia, involved considerable travel to and fro. He found it increasingly wearisome, and now that he was about to contract new familial ties, he had decided to find a quiet country town in which to settle.

He assured me I would love my new home. His eyes shone with the enthusiasm that is his most youthful and attractive characteristic.

"It is a very old town, my dear, founded in the early eighteenth century. Washington was constantly there."

"It seems to me that Washington was everywhere except at home," I said.

Mr. Phelps looked at me in a puzzled way. "But, my

dear," he said mildly, "it was necessary for him to travel a great deal, first as Commander-in-Chief of the American forces during the War of Independence, and then as President. The demands of his office—"

"Of course. I did not mean to be frivolous. Tell me more about General Washington and Stratford."

"He has become such a legend it is difficult to remember that he died—why, it is exactly fifty years ago, in 1799. I talked with residents of Stratford who well remembered his final visit to that city. Mrs. Benjamin Fairchild was able to serve him potatoes from her garden, which he relished very much."

I wonder, I thought to myself, if they still grow potatoes in their gardens, the good people of Stratford. And why should they not? Potatoes are a suitable product for a village garden.

In fact, my first sight of Stratford was a pleasant surprise. The train was not very nice—they make such a noise, and are so very dirty—but the scenery was lovely. Rich meadowland, grand old trees, picturesque vistas crowned by majestic hills, trickling streamlets of pure water running down to the blue waters of the Sound, which sparkled in the spring sunlight. Upon the southern horizon rose the outline of Long Island, which was formerly called Sewanhacky—the Island of Shells—by the Indians who once inhabited this idyllic region. Mr. Phelps, as excited as a boy, told me this fact and others of historical interest. The history of Stratford is as peaceful as its appearance; the bloody skirmishes of war have passed it by, except for encounters with the dusky aborigines. The community's chief claim to fame derives from the visits of General and Mrs. Washington.

Apparently the Great Man's wandering habits were shared by his wife—or else, I mused, she was forever trying to catch up with him! I did not share this whimsy with Mr. Phelps. He would only have looked at me with his puzzled smile. But I suspected I would hear more about the General and his lady than I cared to hear.

Stratford itself was as charming as Mr. Phelps had claimed and not as bucolic as I had feared. It had two churches, a number of shops, and many elegant houses. Our house was on Elm Street, and when the carriage turned into this thoroughfare I found it broad and spacious, lined with fine old trees whose shade was welcome on the warm afternoon. Of course it was not a paved street, one could hardly expect that. But the dwellings of our new neighbors were large and handsome, with wide green lawns that, like our own, stretched down behind the houses to the waters of the Sound.

We had—so Mr. Phelps told me—a property of some three and a half acres. Ideal for the children, I agreed, but I expressed some natural maternal concern about the nearness of the water. Mr. Phelps brushed this aside.

"Henry must learn to swim. It will be good for the boy, you have made him something of a namby-pamby, my dear. Quite natural; but it is time he learned more

162

manly pursuits. As for the younger children, they can hardly get into trouble with you in close attendance, not to mention the servants."

Though the sun had shone brightly during the first part of our journey, clouds gathered as we proceeded. The sullen gray skies were an ominous backdrop for a bride's first vision of her new home.

Yet it was a pleasant house, even under cloudy skies—gleaming with fresh white paint, its facade adorned with a fine portico supported by tall Grecian pillars. Inside, the house was equally immaculate. We had sent servants ahead to prepare for our coming, and, Mr. Phelps said, the good ladies of the congregation had been tireless in their assistance. He had told me little about the place, beyond assuring me that it was elegant and spacious; when I stepped into the hall I suppose my face must have displayed my surprise, for Mr. Phelps smiled.

"Is it not handsome?"

"It is so *long*," I said. "And what a peculiar arrangement for a staircase."

Mr. Phelps stood with his feet apart, viewing the hallway with the fond pride of a new proprietor.

"It was built for a sea captain," he explained. "His wife supervised the construction while he was on his final voyage to China. She did not want him to miss the sea, so she designed the hallway to be exactly the dimensions of a clipper ship's deck—seventy feet long by twelve wide. The twin staircases carry out the same idea of allowing the captain to fancy himself still aboard his beloved ship. After pacing the main deck, he could climb one stair to the hurricane deck, and then descend by the other stair."

"A pretty notion," I said.

And a peculiar notion, I added—but to myself. What is well in a ship does not always suit a house! However, when Harry began running up one staircase and down the other, expressing his loud approval, I was able to contemplate my extraordinary hallway more favorably. It was certainly a splendid place in which to play. Harry gleefully announced his intention of being up and down the stairs all day long. When Mr. Phelps heard this, his expression was decidedly solemn. The room he intended to use as a library was to the right of the stairs. But he said nothing at that time, and I promised myself I would persuade Harry to be considerate of his new papa's need for quiet.

Harry was equally approving of the rest of the house. He declared it was perfect for hide-and-seek, with its many corridors and chambers.

When winter came and the icy winds swept across the Sound, some of the deficiencies of the house became apparent. The drawing room chimney smoked abominably upon occasion, and since this was apparently caused by a certain velocity and direction of wind, nothing could be done about it. The house was a cold house. I was constantly shivering in icy drafts that no one else seemed to feel. Mr. Phelps did not object when I ordered heavier draperies for all the windows and kept the carpenter busy caulking and refitting window frames; but one day in mid-January, when he saw how the woodpile had shrunk, he took me to task for extravagance.

"It is all your imagination, my dear. None of the rest of us is affected by these drafts. You are a little hothouse plant, I am afraid."

I *was* the only one to complain of the cold. But I do not believe now that it was only my imagination.

Mr. Phelps's pastoral duties were not onerous. He was at home a great deal. Snow and freezing weather kept us constantly indoors, and I envied him his ability to amuse himself with one hobby or another. One of his interests, however, caused me some concern as the long months of winter dragged on.

He had never made any particular secret of this interest, but it was not one he advertised abroad. I knew some of his parishioners would not approve of their pastor dabbling with what he called "spiritual philosophy." They would have had other names for it—and so did I. Once I peeped into the journal he had been reading with great interest, and found it was full of references to apparitions and mysterious rappings, phantoms and eerie voices.

I could hardly believe it. I found ghost stories deliciously thrilling—fun to tell on stormy nights by the fire, with good company at hand. But that Mr. Phelps, so serious and so intelligent, could be equally captivated, surprised me. However, when I mentioned the subject to him—I believe I inadvertently used the term "magic"—he was sharp with me.

"I am not concerned with children's fairy tales, Mrs. Phelps, but with unknown science—forces as yet misunderstood by our limited human minds."

"But," I ventured to say, "they speak of the Spirit World, of wonderful messages from the Apostles and the prophets. There was a mother who heard from her little daughter, who had died."

"Ah, that." Mr. Phelps leaned back in his chair. His face took on a dreamy, far-off look. "Imagine hearing, from the lips of St. Luke or Isaiah, a description of the realm of the blessed! The temptation, the well-nigh irresistible lure of that most wonderful of mysteries . . ." His dreamy expression faded, and his voice took on its normal brisk note. "But it is all speculation, there is as yet no real proof that these communications are genuine. Well, my dear, this is a very serious talk for such a little lady. Did you remember to speak to Cook about yesterday's roast? It was sadly overdone. Such a thing must not occur again."

I did not pursue the matter. It sounded rather dull, after all. Another peep into his journal confirmed this impression. There was a long, tedious article on something called Patheticalism, or Pathetism—a means of curing diseases without the use of drugs, which sounded most odd. And although there were many references to goodness and truth and unity, and other admirable qualities, there were few thrilling stories.

So the dull days dragged on. I kept myself busy sewing and playing with the children, and practicing on the piano, which I had sadly neglected in Philadelphia. The ladies of Stratford were assiduous in good works; I served on a dozen committees to educate the heathen and supply them with modest clothing, to call on the sick (who, being of the lower classes, were often rudely unappreciative of the attention), and to improve the lot of servants, children, and fallen women. We did not entertain or go out a great deal. Mr. Phelps seemed more than content, closeted in his library for hours on end.

Then, one February evening, came the event that was to bear such dreadful fruit.

I had been up with the children, helping to tuck them into bed. (There was little else to do in the evening.) After they were snug in their little cots I read them a story and kissed them good night.

Harry was no longer a resident of the nursery. He had firmly announced that he was too old for the company of babies, and had demanded a room of his own. There was no difficulty about that; the house had three floors and a sufficiency of bedchambers. Being older, Harry was allowed to sit up later than the little ones so long as he remained in his room, quietly reading or playing. Usually I went to talk with him for a while after the little ones were in bed. It was for me the best part of the day, and it was all too short. I knew my husband awaited me in the drawing room, and although he usually read to himself and spoke little, he liked me to be there.

That evening there was a change in the routine. As I left the nursery I saw Harry coming along the hall. He was fully dressed.

"Why, Harry," I exclaimed. "What are you doing here? You know Papa said you were to be in your night-gown and in your room at this hour."

Harry gave me a bewitching smile. "It is by his orders that I am freed from prison this evening, Mama. I am to attend him in the library."

"Oh, Harry, have you been naughty again? I begged you—"

"Nothing of the sort." Harry's boyish smile broadened. "I am surprised you have so little faith in me, Mama. I assure you, I am not expecting a beating or a lecture."

"But, Harry—"

"Oh, Mama, don't fuss. You are always fussing."

He scampered away. Filled with the direst forebodings, I started after him. Mr. Phelps may laugh at my premonitions, but I solemnly swear I felt an icy chill run through me. I went after the boy, trying to catch up—all in vain, of course, my stays were too tight to let me breathe deeply, and Harry is very agile when he does not wish to be caught. He was in the best of spirits; he teased me by waiting on the landing till I had almost touched him, and then slipped down one of the twin stairs as I started down the other.

I was pleased to see him merry, but I had cause for concern. Harry had not been well. Physically he seemed in excellent health. Mr. Phelps pointed out, rather smugly, how tall and rosy-cheeked he had grown since we came to Stratford. But his behavior the past few weeks had worried me. It was a kind of nervous excitability. Harry was always volatile—it is the sign of a highly intelligent and artistic character—but of late I fancied his moods were more intense and more rapidly changing. I had had the doctor. He was no help at all. After listening to my description of Harry's behavior, and examining the boy, he had laughed and proclaimed him a thoroughly healthy specimen.

"All he needs, ma'am, is a good touch of the stick. They are limbs of Satan, these young fellows, and they are worse at this time of year when the festivities of the holiday season are over and they see nothing ahead but dreary weather and long months of school. Whack him, ma'am, whack him often and soundly. That will cure his trouble."

Is it any wonder, then, that I was concerned about any unusual mannerism or event where Harry was involved? His spending time with his papa in the library was certainly unusual. As he had indicated, he seldom visited that apartment except for punishment.

Needless to say, I followed him into the room. Mr. Phelps did not appear overly pleased to see me.

"You said you had work to do this evening," he reminded me. "Some sewing task for the Women's Institute that must be finished before tomorrow."

"I have plenty of time," I replied. "You cannot blame me for being curious; what are my two favorite gentlemen planning to do in this mysterious interview?"

"There is nothing mysterious about it," Mr. Phelps said. "I simply saw no reason to mention it to you. Henry has not been himself of late. I have been subjecting him to a course of Pathetic medicine."

"Harry?" I exclaimed. "Medicine? "

Harry threw himself into a big leather chair and crossed his legs. "It is great fun, Mama."

"The term is misleading," Mr. Phelps went on. "There are no drugs or medicines involved. It is a correct Theory of Mind, assisting the spirit to heal itself."

I sat down. "I will help you, Mr. Phelps."

"I hardly think it will interest you, Mrs. Phelps."

"If it is to do with Harry, it will interest me. Pray make allowance, Mr. Phelps, for a mother's natural feelings."

He could not deny me after that. Mr. Phelps has a great deal to say in his sermons and elsewhere about parental love.

I am ashamed to admit what ill-defined fears crowded my mind. I was soon disabused of them; the proceedings were so harmless as to be almost silly. With the room in semidarkness, Mr. Phelps took out his watch and held it before the boy's eyes. In a low, soothing voice he bade him follow the gleaming surface as he moved it gently to and fro.

After a while he said softly, "Can you hear me, Henry?"

"Yes" was the reply, in a voice equally soft.

"How do you feel, my boy?"

"Very calm. Very well."

A few more sentences were exchanged, of the same order. Mr. Phelps kept repeating the words "calm" and "well." Finally he said, "You are calm, you are at peace. You will continue in that state, Henry. Wake now."

Harry rubbed his eyes. "Is it done?"

"Yes, all done. Off to bed now. Sleep well."

"Yes, sir. Good night. Good night, Mama."

When he had gone Mr. Phelps turned to me. "Well, my dear, I trust you are now convinced that I am not abusing the boy."

"I never thought—"

"Lying is a sin, Mrs. Phelps. You suspected me. I confess it hurts me deeply."

In some confusion I apologized, adding, "Indeed, Mr. Phelps, I have never known you to be unkind to anyone. But I don't understand what you were doing. Why did you tell him to wake? He was not asleep. He spoke to you, answered you; his eyes were wide open all the while."

"The process is too complex for you to understand," Mr. Phelps replied. "It is a scientific process. I assure you, I have had considerable experience with it. I employed it on my brother when he suffered from a heart condition, and was able to relieve him greatly."

I know now that the method he employed is called Magnetism, or Mesmerism; it is used, in Pathetic medicine, to put the patient into a proper state of mind. Andrew explained it to me later. When *he* explained, I understood quite well. It is all about vital magnetism and vital electricity, and how one is positive and the other negative. He showed me, with an actual magnet, how the invisible force pulls objects toward the poles. It made very good sense, and it does explain some of the things that happened that spring . . .

Oh, but if that were all—if I could believe there was no other cause. There are doors unseen, opening into unimaginable realms. Once those doors have been opened, what creatures may enter in?

That winter evening I had no such precise fears, only a vague uneasiness. I could hardly forbid the experiments, I had seen nothing to complain of; but the uneasiness persisted, and next day I found myself mentioning the matter to Marian. Ordinarily I do not confide in her, but I knew that any problem involving Harry would touch her.

Like the younger children, she seemed happy in Stratford—as nearly happy as Marian can be. She feels little. She had entered into the various activities of the Ladies' Circle and was constantly busy. Having finished her education the year before, she had nothing else to do except look for a husband, and in that respect, I must confess, I found Stratford somewhat lacking. Marian is not pretty. In order to succeed in what must be any woman's chief endeavor she requires a broad circle of acquaintances. There were few young men of the right age and social position in Stratford. However, Marian did not complain.

She surprised me—it is one of the few times she has succeeded in doing that—when I mentioned Mr. Phelps's treatment of Harry.

"There is no harm in it, Mama. Indeed, I find it beneficial. It is like a pleasant sleep, and one feels so calm afterwards."

"What," I exclaimed. "He has done it to you?"

"He does nothing except assist my own spiritual powers to increase." Marian's thin cheeks were flushed. "I feel much better for it."

"You don't look better for it," I retorted, somewhat sharply. "What have you been doing to yourself? You are thinner than ever and there are shadows under your eyes."

Marian murmured something about sleeping badly.

"If that is all . . . "

"It is nothing serious. I . . . I dream sometimes."

"We all do," I said.

TWENTY-FIVE

NEVER HAS THERE been so long a winter. I was so anxious for spring that tears came to my eyes when I saw the first snowdrops peeking bravely out of the bleak bare earth. But the weather was still chilly and blustery, the trees yet leafless, on that Sunday of March 20, when we prepared for church. The date is, I think, burned forever into the tissue of my brain.

There was the usual Sunday morning bustle. Mr. Phelps was ready first, as usual; as usual, he kept demanding irritably why we could not prepare for this ritual, now so familiar and long-established, without such noise and confusion. Men never understand these things. My first husband was the same. Just let them try to supervise the washing and attiring of four children—

Marian was as bad as the rest, she has no taste in clothes and does not know what to wear—while trying to present a reasonably respectable appearance oneself.

I wore my new suit that morning. It was fine navy blue wool, a trifle light for the season, but I had waited so long for spring; I had to do something to convince myself it was really coming. I had thought the pattern quite pretty when I chose the fabric and the fine braiding that covered the front of the jacket in complex scrolls. However, the final result was somewhat disappointing. The village seamstress has not the fine touch one is accustomed to receiving in a large city.

We got ourselves together and lined up in the hall for inspection, as was our custom. Mr. Phelps confronted us like a general on parade, running his eyes over us one by one. He had no comment for me. I had rather hoped he would say, "Very pretty, my dear," or something of that sort.

Marian, too, passed without criticism, though I thought her appearance quite dreadful; the dull maroon of her gown made her skin sallower than ever. Harry was subjected to a scathing critique. Everything was wrong, from his uncombed hair to his scuffed boots. The little ones, whom I held firmly, one in each hand, won a fatherly pat on the head.

We took the carriage, since the weather threatened, though the distance was short. Harry had to sit on the box with the coachman, which he did not mind at all.

I do not recall the text or the sermon. I do remember

that Harry was restless—not unusually restless, no more than normal for a boy his age. Since the pastoral pew is just under the pulpit, his actions did not go unnoticed, and I was constantly having to nudge and frown at him.

It is a wonder I remember anything of that frightful day except the event that turned it into nightmare—the beginning of a long and continuing evil dream.

It always took us forever to get away after the service. Mr. Phelps must talk with everyone who wanted to chat. He insisted that we wait with him, which was difficult for the children. When we got into the carriage, the three younger ones behaved like little animals let out of their cages. Harry was not the only one in high spirits; Willy pinched his sister, who slapped him and burst into tears. Mr. Phelps exclaimed, as he frequently did, "One would think they had come from a zoological garden instead of a house of God!"

Everything was as usual. Nothing was different . . . until we reached home.

A cold drizzling rain had begun to fall. Anxious not to damage my new suit, I hastened toward the house. My entrance was facilitated for me, in no pleasant way. The front door stood wide open.

I stood staring at it rather stupidly until the others joined me on the portico. Marian had the smaller children by the hand. Harry was close behind her, followed by his papa.

"Why do you not go in?" Mr. Phelps inquired.

I gestured. "The door. Did you forget to close it?"

"Certainly not. I thought you—"

"No, it was like that when I came up."

Mr. Phelps frowned. "I won't tolerate this sort of thing. Come along, Mrs. Phelps, we must have a word with the servants."

He strode into the house. One can almost measure Mr. Phelps's temper by the length of his strides. I followed, plucking at his sleeve. It was difficult enough to find decent servants in a small town. I did not want them upset unnecessarily.

"But, Mr. Phelps, the servants were at church. Nor would they have occasion to use this door."

"All the same, they must be questioned."

Naturally, the servants one and all denied being responsible. They had returned from church before us, on foot; but had used the back entrance and had not even gone into the front part of the house. The only exception was Cook, who had, of course, remained at home to complete the preparations for dinner. No one could suspect her; she was the most respectable of middle-aged females, and her indignation at being accused, even by implication, was obviously genuine. Even more convincing of her innocence was the terror that replaced her initial outrage.

"Burglars! That's what it was, criminals and burglars. We'll be murdered in our beds, we will. I won't stay in this house another minute!"

Having aroused this storm, Mr. Phelps left me to calm it, and it required some time to convince Cook that she was not in mortal danger—particularly when I was not too easy in my own mind. After leaving the kitchen I found Mr. Phelps in the hall, about to mount the stairs.

"The doors to the library and morning room were also open," he said. "I am sure I closed the former, as I always do."

"Was that all?"

"It is enough to indicate that someone has been in the house. I am now about to examine the upper chambers."

We went from room to room without finding anything amiss until we reached our own bedroom. Mr. Phelps preceded me. When he looked in, he uttered a loud exclamation.

"What is it, what is it?" I cried apprehensively.

Silently he stood aside. When I saw what had prompted his cry, my relief was so great I could have laughed aloud. Four chairs had been piled on top of our bed, their wooden legs forming a weird tangle.

Mr. Phelps did not share my relief. In the low, stern voice that characterizes his angrier moods he said, "Mischief. Some trickster has done this."

And he turned to direct a cold, hostile gaze upon Harry, who, hearing our voices and sharing our concern, had come to see what was happening.

Observing the strange construction on the bed, Harry burst out laughing. Indeed, I could not blame him, but the effect was unfortunate. Mr. Phelps's face darkened. Before he could speak, I said quickly, "It could not have been Harry. He was with us the entire time."

"He could have done this before we left the house," Mr. Phelps said.

"But he could not have opened the front door. You yourself closed it when we left, and you were the last to get into the carriage."

Harry's smile had faded. His quick intelligence needed no direct accusation to realize he was under suspicion.

"I didn't do it," he cried. "Honestly—"

"This is a serious matter, Henry," Mr. Phelps said. "Give me your word that you know nothing of this."

"Honestly, Papa—"

"Very well, very well. I believe you."

It cannot be said that Sunday dinner was a pleasant meal. Cook's perturbation had resulted in another badly cooked joint, and the housemaid was so nervous she dropped two plates. Marian looked like a ghost. Harry continued to speculate and wonder about the strange events until his papa cut him short.

"The miscreants are probably mischievous boys," he said firmly. "As you know, Henry, I do not approve of some of your friends. No, do not interrupt me, I am not blaming you or doubting that you are ignorant of these tricks; I am simply saying that some of your associates might consider this sort of thing humorous. Let us hear no more about it. I will take steps to prevent its happening again."

When dinner was over we went upstairs to prepare for the afternoon service. Mr. Phelps did not come up; he had gone to the library. When I was ready I went to look for him and found, to my surprise, that he was stretched out on the sofa reading.

"You will be late," I said.

"I am not going."

"But—"

"As you know, I do not preach this afternoon. I mean to stay here and keep watch, in case those bad boys try to play another trick."

He had deliberately delayed telling me this, I knew, in order to prevent Harry from warning his friends. He still suspected my boy, despite the lad's solemn oath. I was very much wounded. Without speaking to him again I left the room; and I cannot say that the halting utterances of the assistant pastor helped to soothe my injured spirit.

Of course I said nothing to Harry of his papa's unfair suspicions, and my boy was his cheery self, grumbling as usual about the necessity of attending church, not once but twice in a day. The rain had stopped when we returned, but the clouds still hovered, and when we entered the house I saw with considerable irritation that the servants had not yet lit the lamps. Mr. Phelps was still in the library. He sat up with a start when I entered. It was too dark for me to see his face, but I felt certain he had been napping.

"Has anything happened?" I demanded. I hoped it had. Harry had been with me every second. A further outbreak of mischief during our absence would prove his innocence.

"It has been completely quiet," said Mr. Phelps, trying to hide a yawn.

In some bitterness of spirit I summoned the housemaid and told her to light the lamps. Taking a candle, I started up the stairs. Mr. Phelps came out of the library and followed, but I was so annoyed I did not turn to speak to him, or wait for him to open the door of our room.

My candle died, extinguished by the icy draft issuing from the opening doors. The fire burned low, cloaking the room with shadows. In the reddish glow I saw what lay on our bed—a motionless and dreadful form, shrouded for the grave.

The candle dropped from my nerveless hand. A black mist threatened to envelop me. As I swayed, I felt my husband's hands support me. His sharp intake of breath, like a muffled cry, told me the terrible vision was not the product of my imagination.

Thrusting me unceremoniously aside, he ran to the bed. I let out a shriek when his hands touched the silent form. But worse was to come. With a muffled sound, more like an animal's growl than a human voice, Mr. Phelps began to dismember the corpse. Its head flew in one direction, its body in another.

I remember nothing more until I woke, my nostrils quivering with the sting of smelling salts, to find myself lying on that same bed.

The shock to my system was so extreme that I feel it yet. Before I could spring shrieking from that infernal couch, Mr. Phelps spoke.

"It was only a dummy, made of clothing wrapped in a sheet. For the love of heaven, calm yourself, Mrs. Phelps."

But it was the voice of my dear boy that saved my reason. Tears streaming down his face, he clutched my hand and implored me not to die—for as he told me, so deadly was my pallor that he feared me on the brink of extinction.

"Dearest Harry, Mama will not die," I assured him. "I was only startled for a moment. I am well now."

"You would not do such a thing to frighten your Mama, would you, Henry?" Mr. Phelps asked.

I clutched my boy to my bosom. "Harry was with me all afternoon, you know that. How you dare—"

"Very well! You are quite right and I own I am wrong. Are you recovered now? I must investigate and see what other mischief has occurred."

"My bed has been pulled out into the middle of the room," Harry volunteered in a voice still choked with sobs. "And Marian said her small inlaid table is missing."

His face shone with tears. He gazed up at his papa with wide, luminous eyes. I had never seen anyone so palpably innocent. Even Mr. Phelps was moved.

"It is all very curious," he muttered. "I cannot account for it, unless . . . But no, that cannot be. Stay with your mama, Henry, and take care of her."

But Harry was understandably wild with curiosity to see what else had happened, and I forced myself to rise and accompany him. Close examination of the house produced some amazing discoveries. Marian's inlaid table had been crammed into her wardrobe, crushing her frocks. Several other pieces of furniture were disarranged or hidden; and loud outcries from the kitchen proved to result from Cook's discovery that the loaf of bread she had set out for tea had disappeared. It was eventually found in the morning room in a bookcase.

It was late evening before order was restored and the children sent to bed. I lingered long with them, afraid to leave them alone. Finally Mr. Phelps sent one of the maids to summon me to the library.

He had little to say, however. He spent most of the evening turning through various newspapers, as if in search of some particular article. When I tried to speak of the horrors that had occurred, he was brusque with me.

"I am taking steps, Mrs. Phelps. You need not concern yourself."

I did not go up before him, as I sometimes did. I could not have entered that room alone. Only with an extreme effort of will did I force myself to take my place beside him in the bed. In the darkness I felt the presence of the shrouded corpse between us.

TWENTY-SIX

MY **FIRST THOUGHT** on waking next morning was to rush to my children. Nothing had occurred during the night; however, Harry looked at me in surprise when I asked if he was all right, and replied grumpily that he was not, for this was Monday and a long week of school stretched ahead of him. He added that he felt sure the Lord had not made Monday; some Other Power must have been responsible.

This was reassuring. The sight of Marian at the breakfast table was less so. She crumbled her food instead of eating and looked as if she had not slept a wink. Mr. Phelps noticed her distraction. After Harry had left for school he said, "Come to me in the library, Marian, and we will have another treatment."

"If Marian is ill perhaps we ought to have the doctor," I said listlessly.

"You yourself informed me, Mrs. Phelps, that the man was an ignorant, sadistic quack."

"Did I? Well, Mr. Phelps, I am sure you know best."

So they went off together and I busied myself with the normal morning chores. I was in the parlor, dusting the china ornaments, which I prefer not to leave to the clumsy hands of the maids, when I heard a scream from the floor above.

As I entered the hall Mr. Phelps came out of the library. The screams had stopped but had been replaced by wild shuddering sobs that were almost as loud.

"Marian?" I asked.

"She has just left me."

The screams had indeed been uttered by my daughter. She was in a full-fledged fit of hysteria when we found her, standing in the open door of her room. Its condition gave some excuse for her distress. The furniture was strewn about in utter confusion. The washstand, normally concealed behind a screen, stood blatantly in the center of the room with the towels draped over it. Next to the washstand was a trunk, one of the humpbacked type bound in brass, in which Marian stored extra clothing. Its lid had been tipped back, and atop the neatly folded garments was a heap of masculine clothing—trousers, vest, coat—which I at once recognized as belonging to Mr. Phelps.

He had to raise his voice to be heard over Marian's sobs.

"Those are the garments that were used last night to create the form on our bed," he cried. "How did they come here?"

The uncouth gulping sounds coming from Marian scratched at my nerves, which, needless to say, were in a dreadful state. Turning, I slapped her sharply on the cheek. This is, of course, the best cure for hysteria, and it had the desired effect. Marian's sobbing ended. Her hand at her burning cheek, she looked at me in shocked surprise. I had never struck her before. I do not believe in striking children.

"It was necessary," I said, in answer to her wordless reproach. "Are you better now? Sit down—breathe deeply—and tell me what has happened."

Marian obeyed, jerkily, like a puppet. Still holding her cheek, she shook her head. "I found it . . . like this."

"These garments." Mr. Phelps held them out.

"They are yours, are they not, Papa?" Marian looked bewildered. "I don't know how they came here."

Mr. Phelps tossed them back into the trunk. "This is beyond words."

"You cannot accuse Harry," I cried. "He—"

"He could have done this before he left for school. Marian is always early to breakfast and he is invariably late." Hands clasped behind his back, Mr. Phelps walked around the room, peering closely at the disarranged furniture. I found myself doing the same, as if hoping some solution would suddenly leap out at me— a solution that would clear my boy, once and forever.

Suddenly there was another shriek from Marian. So overwrought was I that I echoed it. Whirling around, I saw her bolt upright in her chair, her arm outstretched, her finger pointing.

"The clothing," she gasped. "It is gone."

Sure enough, the suit of gentleman's clothes was no longer in the trunk. Marian began babbling. "I had covered my face with my hands—when I took them away, the things were gone—"

"Hush," I exclaimed. "Be still or I will slap you again. Dear Heaven, I cannot endure any more of this."

Again Mr. Phelps searched the room, this time to more purpose. The missing garments were found under the bed.

At this discovery Marian began weeping noisily. I jumped at her and shook her by the shoulders. It was not such a terrible thing to do, and I do not remember crying out; but Mr. Phelps said I was losing control of myself.

"I will put the clothes away," he said sternly. "Be assured this time they will stay there!"

Flinging the garments into the trunk, he carried it into the closet, which he locked. He ushered us from the room, then turned the key in the lock and did the same for the communicating door to the next room.

"There," he said, putting the keys in his pocket. "Now we will see."

Marian crept away, looking like a red-nosed, fright

ened mouse. I felt I must lie down. I ought to have been relieved. Harry could hardly be accused of hiding the garments under the bed. But I was shaking uncontrollably. How had the suit of clothing—which I devoutly hoped Mr. Phelps would never wear again—how had it moved from the trunk to the floor, and under the bed? Marian might have moved it, while Mr. Phelps and I were looking elsewhere. But why should she do such a mad thing? And she had certainly appeared to be as alarmed as we ...

Had Mr. Phelps really been alarmed? Men must conceal their fears, if they feel them; but the more I thought about it, the more I suspected that his eyes had held a strange glint, a look, almost, of pleasurable excitement.

I decided that I must have been mistaken. That was the last emotion one would expect to see in a man so tormented.

Shortly I heard his footsteps approach the door, which had been left ajar. To my surprise—for I had expected he would come to inquire how I felt—the steps did not pause, but went on past. They were very quiet, as if he were tiptoeing.

The most incredible surmises troubled my mind. Rising, I went to the door and peered out.

Mr. Phelps stood by Marian's door. As I watched, unobserved, he took a key from his pocket and inserted it into the lock. I heard the sharp click as it turned. Gingerly he opened the door.

The sound he made was not a gasp of surprise, but a

long, drawn-out "ah!" He smiled. It was a dreadful smile, a sinister smile. I could bear the suspense no longer. I ran to his side.

On the floor of Marian's room, just inside the door, lay the suit of clothes which, scarcely fifteen minutes before, he had locked in the closet of that locked room.

TWENTY-SEVEN

I WAS PITIABLY SHAKEN. Indeed, I remember very little of what transpired thereafter until I found myself entering the library, leaning on Mr. Phelps's arm. After he had placed me in a chair he insisted I take a small glass of port, which was kept on hand for medicinal purposes. He was kind in his way, but when I asked that the maid be sent for a cup of tea, he refused.

"I don't want servants brought into this until it is unavoidable. They are a superstitious, ignorant lot and will take fright."

I did not reply in words; but my glance, I believe, was eloquent. Mr. Phelps shook his head, almost playfully. I could not understand his mood.

"My dear Mrs. Phelps, I assure you there is nothing

to fear. I may be excused in the beginning for failing to understand the truth; but the events of this morning puts the question beyond doubt. To think that I have seen with my own eyes phenomena I have often read about and often doubted!"

He went on in this dreadful vein of self-congratulation until I interrupted with a demand for an explanation. If my tone was somewhat shrill, I think that is excusable.

"I was reading just last night of a similar case," Mr. Phelps said. "Have you not heard of the Rochester rappings? The newspapers have been full of them for months."

He then went on to explain, in his most tedious and pedantic manner. It seems that for some time two young women (they were of an inferior social class, so one can hardly call them young ladies) named Fox, in a small town in New York, had been producing raps and scratching sounds out of thin air. Some invisible intelligence was obviously responsible for the sounds, since it responded to questions, rapping for "yes," remaining silent for "no," and spelling out more complete answers by rapping when the correct letter of the alphabet was reached by a person reciting it. That the phenomenon was connected with the Fox sisters, and not with the house in which they lived, was proved by the fact that when the girls went elsewhere, the rapping broke out in those places also. Other persons had taken up the sport of calling on these invisible "spirits"—the word is that of Mr. Phelps—and had received answers to the most compelling theological questions.

Mr. Phelps would have gone on and on about the wretched girls and their raps if I had not interrupted.

"What has this to do with us? We have heard no—"

"Do you remember last Tuesday, when the door knocker sounded and the housemaid reported no one was there?"

"Some mischievous child. You said so yourself."

"I was mistaken. Phenomena such as we observed this morning, and also yesterday, are well known. Ignorant persons attribute them to ghosts, or 'haunts'; until recently educated persons dismissed them as pure imagination. We now have reason to suspect they are demonstrations of some unknown force."

"A diabolical force," I cried.

"I cannot deny that possibility." Mr. Phelps looked grave. "But I assure you, there is nothing to fear so long as we remain calm, and secure in our faith. Who knows, we may have seen the last of these demonstrations already."

"Oh, I hope so!"

But I was not convinced by his explanation. Having denied, at first, the possibility of trickery, for fear Harry would be accused, I now clung to that theory as to a lifeline. It must be Marian who was responsible. I did not ask myself why she might have done such things, I only persuaded myself that she might have been able to do them, and promised myself a firm talk with her. However, when I expressed this intention to Mr. Phelps (without elaborating on my true reasons for wishing to do so), he forbade me to see her—my own daughter!

"She is in an extremely nervous state, Mrs. Phelps. I took the opportunity of giving her another treatment of Pathetism, and she is now resting. Pray do not disturb her."

And, as it turned out, such a talk would have been unnecessary. That afternoon it was proved, beyond a shadow of a doubt, that neither Marian nor any other living creature was responsible for the terrors that afflicted us.

I did not see the first of the occurrences, but I heard the housemaid cry out. She was in the hall. Upon being questioned, she insisted that Mr. Phelps's umbrella had hurtled past her, half the length of the hall. There was no one else in the room.

Scarcely had Mr. Phelps succeeded in calming the girl when the door knocker sounded, and so stretched were our nerves that even Mr. Phelps started visibly. But upon opening the door we beheld nothing more alarming than little Mrs. Platts, the music teacher, who had come to give Harry his lesson.

Naturally I tried to behave as if nothing were amiss. Mrs. Platts is the worst gossip in Stratford, and I did not want her telling tales all over town. I called up to Harry—a reluctant musician at best, he was skulking in his room—and showed Mrs. Platts into the music room. Eventually I had to call to Marian and ask her to fetch her brother, which she did. Mr. Phelps's treatment appeared to have helped her. She looked more alert than she had done for some days.

It was necessary to spend some time chatting with Mrs. Platts, for Mr. Phelps insisted we treat her like the distressed gentlewoman she claimed to be. He made a point of coming in to greet her himself. We were talking idly when Mrs. Platts let out a cry and put her hand to her head. I had not been looking directly at her. Mr. Phelps had. With the agility of a man half his age he sprang to her side and picked up a hairbrush from the floor beside her.

"Are you hurt?" he inquired.

Mrs. Platts rubbed her head. "No, it was not a hard rap. I am sorry; I fear I must have knocked the brush from—er—its former place."

This was patently impossible, the only piece of furniture within arm's reach of Mrs. Platts being a low table. If the brush had been on it, it would simply have fallen to the floor instead of rising in the air and striking her on the head.

I saw at once where her suspicions lay. She could not keep her eyes from Harry, who was standing on the other side of the room as far from the piano as he could get.

Mrs. Platts rose and went to the fire, rubbing her hands together and remarking on the chill of the day. Scarcely had she left her chair when there was a loud, discordant crash from the piano. It sounded as if half a dozen of its strings had been violently snapped. Mrs. Platts squealed. Under other circumstances I might have been hard pressed not to laugh, she looked so comical, with her large mouth ajar and her eyes bulging.

The first thing was to open the piano. Mr. Phelps did so with Harry's assistance. Reaching inside, he lifted out a large block of wood and stood weighing it in his hands.

"Has it damaged the strings?" Harry inquired hopefully.

"That is hardly the vital question," Mr. Phelps replied.

"But if the piano is broken I cannot have my lesson," Harry insisted.

Mrs. Platts was suddenly galvanized into action. "Quite right. The instrument should be tested before . . . This is not a proper time . . . You will excuse me, I hope, I have just remembered . . . No, no, you need not show me to the door, I will . . ." And she departed, uttering fragmentary sentences that sounded like sharp little shrieks of consternation.

I had been watching Harry. I had seen his hand move, just before Mrs. Platts cried out.

But if *he* had thrown the brush, who had moved the block of wood through a closed lid and dropped it violently onto the piano wires?

It was too much for me. I managed to retain control of myself until Mrs. Platts had gone. Then I slid to the floor in a dead faint.

TWENTY-EIGHT

I KEPT TO MY BED next morning. I suppose it was childish—like hiding one's head under the covers—and if I had hoped thus to escape knowledge of new horrors, I was not allowed. Soon after breakfast Harry came running in to announce that further manifestations had occurred during prayers. He had been struck on the head by a key, and various objects, including a tin box, had been propelled across the room by invisible hands. When I demanded why he was not at school, he snuffled unconvincingly and said Papa had agreed he was coming down with a cold.

Mr. Phelps did not visit me until later in the morning. I saw at once, by his face, that he had more news—bad news.

"I have just found a cloth spread on the floor, with a Bible and three candlesticks arranged—"

"I don't want to hear about it."

"You must get up, however. I have asked the Reverend Dr. Mitchell to spend the day, in the hope of getting his advice."

I protested. He was adamant.

"There is no chance of keeping these things secret any longer. I kept Henry at home to prevent him from gossiping to his friends, but he cannot remain secluded indefinitely. Besides, Mrs. Platts has undoubtedly told her tale to half the town. We owe it to ourselves to have the testimony of a man such as Reverend Mitchell."

"His wife dislikes me. She will revel in—"

"In what, for heavens sake? Our misfortune? I cannot believe anyone would be so uncharitable. Now, Mrs. Phelps, you must calm yourself. Your present state alarms me. I have been thinking you might profit from the treatments I have been giving Marian and Henry."

I was too weak and disheartened to protest.

It was the strangest experience. Apprehensive at first of I knew not what, I felt the most exquisite drowsiness gradually seize me as my eyes followed the slow swinging of his watch. After that it seemed but an instant before I was wide awake, with no recollection of any passage of time. Mr. Phelps sat on the side of the bed regarding me with a puzzled look, the same one I had often seen on his face when I tried to make a little joke.

"What is it?" I asked dazedly.

"Do you remember anything you said?"

"I don't remember speaking at all. What did—"

"Do you feel better?"

"I do. I feel more at ease."

"Good." Mr. Phelps rose. "You will come down for dinner, I trust. Mr. Mitchell will join us at the meal and remain for the rest of the day."

Without the treatment I am convinced I could never have endured the distress of Mr. Mitchell's presence. A tall, severe-looking gentleman, he had always treated me with reserve, and as my husband narrated the strange events that had perplexed us, his cold gray eyes kept wandering in my direction as if to say, "There is the culprit."

But I was vindicated. During dinner Mr. Mitchell was treated to the spectacle of knives and forks and other objects flying around the dining room. No sooner had his astonished eyes turned to follow one than another hurtled past him. One spoon struck him with a thump on top of his bald head; and I had to stifle a laugh.

Mr. Mitchell returned—for you can be sure he was there early the following morning—and by 4:00 P.M. we had counted over forty-five different objects that had been moved, some of them several times. On Thursday another clergyman, Mr. Weed, was asked to be present. This was the first time we heard noises like the rappings Mr. Phelps had mentioned to me. Some of them were produced by a brass candlestick, which beat itself against the floor until it finally broke.

It was also on this day that the mysterious writings first appeared. They were scratched onto a turnip, of all the unlikely things, which was thrown through the parlor window; and Mr. Weed's bushy gray eyebrows rose clear up into his hair when this object was handed to him.

I could go on for many pages describing the other objects that moved, including the heavy mahogany dining room table. The writings continued to materialize, often on the most bizarre objects. Harry's cap, pantaloons, and blue silk handkerchief were so adorned. I could only shake my head helplessly when they were shown to me. The characters were like none I had ever seen before, and the clergymen, familiar with such esoteric scripts as Greek and Hebrew, said the same.

By that time we suffered what I privately called a plague of pastors. Not only Mr. Mitchell and Mr. Weed, but several other gentlemen of the cloth, from Stratford and even nearby towns, had been summoned to assist us in our trouble. This was Mr. Mitchell's idea. He even went so far as to remark, in his pompous manner, that if there were evil spirits in the house, the presence of so many servants of God ought to intimidate them.

Quite the contrary. The reverend gentlemen inspired more outrageous outbursts than before. Objects continued to whiz around the house and the large knocker of the outside door sounded constantly, without any human agency having touched it. The most annoying new trick was played in the pantry. One morning all its contents were tossed into the kitchen, bags of salt and sugar emptied onto the promiscuous heap of tinware and culinary instruments. Cook threatened again to leave and was persuaded to stay on only by promises of extravagant rises in salary.

If I seem to speak lightly of these matters, it is because I realize that in retrospect some of them seem frivolous, almost amusing—tricks played by a naughty child, annoying but basically harmless. The most curious thing of all was that in a surprisingly short time we became almost accustomed to them. I am told that this is not, in fact, surprising; that the human constitution can adjust to an astonishing variety of experiences, and that an act repeated often enough becomes a custom, and thereby endurable. Mr. Phelps's calm was assisted by what I was forced to regard as morbid, unhealthy curiosity. He was visibly affected by the strange phenomena; they troubled him greatly, yet under his serious looks and frowning brow I often saw his eyes gleam as he ran from room to room, notebook in hand, jotting down memoranda of what was transpiring.

Needless to say, I had no such aid. Mr. Phelps's treatments may have helped me to remain calm—I do not claim they did not—but I believe the only reason I was not in a constant state of hysteria was that my nerves had become numbed, as after a mortal shock.

Even now, my memory misbehaves, in the most inconsistent fashion. Some of the events of those terrible months are already blurred and indistinct, like recollections of the distant past. Others stand out in shocking clarity, the colors as bright, the sounds as distinct, as when I experienced the event. One of the latter is particularly vivid in my mind. It was, if not the most frightening, the most awesome and bizarre of all our experiences.

It occurred during the period when the inquisitive clergymen were with us. Mr. Mitchell had decided that they must keep a constant watch on all parts of the house. So they rushed from room to room, up and down the stairs and along the passageways, looking for all the world like a swarm of very large somber beetles in their dark suits and spectacles. It was unnerving in the extreme. I would be sitting with my embroidery in the morning room, trying to snatch a few moments of peace, when a clerical head would appear around the door frame and a pair of glittering eyeglasses would stare at me. I daresay it sounds very amusing. The culmination of the experiment was anything but that.

The gentlemen had determined one day to subject the house to a rigorous search, from cellar to attic. Heaven knows what they hoped to find—an infernal machine of some kind, perhaps, or confederates of ours, hiding in dark corners and waiting for an opportunity to play another trick. While they were busy with this I decided to retire to my room, hoping that this sanctum at least would be free from their investigations.

Marian's room, as I believe I have indicated, was down the hall from the room of myself and Mr. Phelps. As I entered the corridor I saw her standing by her open door.

She turned very slowly to look at me. I scarcely recognized her. Though her body was quite still, her arms hanging limply at her sides, her entire countenance quivered and twitched, as if every muscle in it had been subjected to a violent shock.

"Mama," she said quietly. "Come and see this."

My involuntary cry of surprise brought my husband running. He summoned the others. Before long there was a sizable audience. The word is appropriate; the scene before us resembled nothing so much as a tableau, or a setting for a theatrical performance, complete with actors.

Most of the furniture had been pushed aside—a task requiring no small strength in itself. In the space thus cleared a number of figures had been arranged, in the most graceful and lifelike attitudes. They were formed from articles of clothing, padded out to resemble human forms. Most were female figures—the garments were both mine and Marian's—in attitudes of devotion. Some knelt before open Bibles. Others were crouched, their "faces" bent to the floor in poses of extreme humility.

In the center of the floor squatted a strange, dwarfish figure whose basic constituent was poor little Willy's best Sunday suit; but this had been so grotesquely adorned with artificial flowers and ribbons and other feminine articles that it resembled something out of a madman's nightmare. This was, however, the only ugly or repulsive figure; it almost seemed as though the lovely women's shapes guarded it, turning to devout prayer as a means of shielding the dwellers in the house from the malice such misshapen creatures are known to feel. This impression was strengthened by the last figure, which was suspended from the ceiling as if flying through the air, or hovering in benediction above the worshippers.

The whole ensemble was so strange and yet so picturesque that we were struck dumb. I cannot emphasize too strongly the lifelike appearance of the attitudes. The unknown arranger had been fiendishly clever in setting them up in such a way that the blank stuffed faces were turned away or hidden. One figure, fashioned from a gown of my own, knelt gracefully by the bed. I did not recognize the gown at first, it was an old one I had not worn for some time, and my first impression was only one of vague familiarity: "Where have I seen that woman before?" Then, behind me, I heard my little Willy whisper to his sister, "Ma is saying her prayers." And I knew the gown and the figure were my own.

Until that moment I had not been conscious of fear. Awe and amazement were the predominant emotions in every breast, for the tableau was as beautiful and impressive as it was strange. But when I recognized the kneeling woman's form, an icy chill pervaded my limbs. I remembered the old legend of the doppelgänger, or double. To recognize such a figure, the precise replica of oneself, is an omen of sudden death.

One of the clergymen was the first to break the awed silence.

"We ought to take a copy of this. A sketch."

It was a sensible suggestion, but no one moved to follow it. Mr. Weed murmured, "No need; I doubt that any of us will forget it."

He, I might add, was later to say the most insulting things about us, claiming he had seen nothing a three-year-old child could not have done and implying that we ourselves had played tricks on him and the other clergymen. He referred, disparagingly, to the scene I have just described as "images or dolls dressed up the size of life." All I can say is that at the time he was as dumbfounded as the rest of us.

Everyone in the house, including the unfortunate servants, was subjected to a cross-examination. It was impossible to prove that each and every person had been under observation the entire day, but even Mr. Weed admitted that he could not see how the ensemble had been created. Not a sound had been heard, not a person had been seen running to and fro with armfuls of clothing; and since the garments, the Bibles, and other objects had been gathered from all over the house, the construction of the chapel scene, as my husband termed it, must have taken long hours of labor. As Mr. Webster said, "No three women could have done it in as many hours, much less without attracting attention and eliciting suspicion by their rapid movements."

"And," Mr. Mitchell added, rubbing his bald head in perplexity, "we were all on the *qui vive* the entire day, looking for evidence of trickery. I can swear, gentlemen, that I saw nothing the whole time."

TWENTY-NINE

I HAD NOT VENTURED from the house since that awful Sunday. By the end of the week the weather cleared and Mr. Phelps insisted I do the marketing, as much for the exercise as the duty itself. I was not reluctant to leave the house. Mr. Mitchell and Mr. Webster were still prowling about getting in everyone's way. Mr. Weed had, quite suddenly, taken his departure, with unconvincing excuses of pressing business which he had not seen fit to mention earlier. It was obvious that the situation had gotten beyond him. A man of limited imagination and narrow mind, unable to believe what he had seen yet unable to deny the evidence of his own senses, he sought refuge in flight. Later, as I have said, he denied that there was anything extraordinary in the case. Perhaps by that time he had managed to convince himself that he spoke the truth.

Even after my morning treatment from Mr. Phelps, on which I had come to rely, I contemplated the trip into town with some apprehension. Men do not understand. They cannot realize the cruelties women inflict on their fellow women. The sidelong glance, the sly little smile, the seemingly harmless comments that raise smarting welts . . .

I knew what the good ladies of the church thought of me; I had overheard a few remarks others had made—kindly passed on to me by "friends." "Too young," "too frivolous," "he was mad to take on the responsibility of a family at his age . . . ," "and such a family . . . the boy, they say, is quite wild."

The road was muddy from the recent rains. I had to keep to the grass verge. The walk itself was pleasant enough. The trees had fat, promising buds all along their limbs and some of the lawns boasted brave displays of crocuses and an occasional courageous daffodil.

My rising spirits received a rude check when I reached the shops and saw that the ladies of the town were out in full force. It was the first fine day for almost a week, and they were starved for gossip. Even Mrs. Mitchell was there, the center of an avidly listening group. She usually left the shopping to her servants—and was roundly cheated in consequence. This morning some stronger impulse had conquered her laziness; and I doubted that it was the spring sunshine.

Mrs. Platts was the focus of another circle. If I had

entertained any doubts as to the subject of the discussion, they would have been dissipated by Mrs. Platts's reaction when she saw me approach. She broke off speaking, her hand flew to her mouth, her eyes widened. With a false smile and a nod in my general direction, she turned and fled.

I tried to act as usual, nodding and smiling as I walked on. They had not the effrontery to question me directly—not then. There were murmurs of "How are you feeling, Mrs. Phelps?" and "I had heard you were unwell, Mrs. Phelps," to which I replied as casually as I could. By the time I reached the shop door my hands were shaking, and I was vastly relieved to find that the only customer at the counter was old Mrs. Babcock, who was avoided by the other ladies because her sole topic of conversation was the fifty-year-old visit of Mrs. and General Washington. I had heard the story myself at least a dozen times, and had vowed I would never listen to it again. This morning I actually raised the subject myself, to prevent Mrs. Babcock from mentioning other matters.

Even she failed me. Properly nudged, she rambled on for a time about Mrs. Washington's chariot, drawn by four white horses ridden by black postilions in scarlet and white livery with white cockades in their hats. But the spreading gossip had penetrated even her senile brain. She broke off in the middle of a sentence to inquire, with the rudeness old ladies feel entitled to display, "What is going on at the parsonage, Mrs. Phelps? I have heard the most peculiar stories about all of you."

I don't remember what I said. When I finally reached home I found I had purchased red ribbons instead of blue, and had forgotten the buttons for Harry's trousers.

Even now I break out into a cold perspiration when I think of it. In some ways it was the hardest part of the whole affair. I did not see how I could go on.

Then the miracle happened. Andrew came. Like an angel of mercy bearing a heavenly message, he rescued me from my torment.

I smile, though sadly, when I remember how casually I responded to the first mention of his name. Of course, I did not know who he was. When I heard of his projected visit he seemed like another of the ghouls who came to feed their horrid curiosity on our suffering.

Nothing spreads so fast as gossip, and malicious gossip has a demonic life all its own; it appears to die in one spot and springs up, without apparent cause, in a dozen others. I am not certain how the word of our troubles reached so rapidly beyond the confines of Stratford. One would think that a clergyman's principles would prevent him from telling tales to his wife and friends, but I am no longer so naive as to believe that; I suspect Mr. Phelps wrote to some of the acquaintances who shared his interest in spiritualist matters. I could hardly believe he would do such a thing, but the promptness with which these vultures gathered was highly indicative.

I protested, as vigorously as my highly nervous condition allowed, when Mr. Phelps informed me we would be entertaining certain newspaper persons.

"It is our duty to science to report these happenings," he said solemnly. "Be realistic, Mrs. Phelps. The story will spread no matter what we do. Is it not common sense to make sure that what is printed is the truth, instead of superstitious fancies?"

He had a way of putting things that made it impossible for me to disagree with him. My feelings told me he was wrong, but gentlemen do not have much regard for a woman's feelings.

So, once the plague of clergymen had passed, the second plague, of newspaper reporters, descended upon us. At one time or another we had representatives of the *New Haven Journal and Courier*, the *Derby Journal*, and the *Bridgeport Standard*. There was even a person from one of the New York papers, his name was Beach, or Shore, or something of that sort. And never did our invisible tormentors fail to entertain them.

I actually developed a certain liking for one of the reporters, Mr. Newson, of the *Derby Journal*. He was a nice-looking young fellow, with thoughtful brown eyes and a modest manner. His newspaper—I was told—has a much more limited circulation than the others, so his professional position is inferior in consequence, I suppose. I don't think that fact accounts for his good manners, however. He seemed a naturally kind-hearted and sympathetic man, and his unfailing courtesy to me, as well as his instinctive comprehension of the difficulties of my position, could not fail to make a good impression on me. I particularly appreciated his taking me aside, soon after his arrival, to assure me that he hoped I would not misunderstand the precautions he and the others felt it necessary to take.

"It does not imply the slightest suspicion of anyone, Mrs. Phelps," he said earnestly. "It is the usual procedure, I assure you. I would feel obliged to do the same if the President of the United States were involved."

It is strange, is it not, how distinctly I remember this speech and the young man's pleasant appearances when I have forgotten so much? I am not sure what other persons were present on that occasion—there were a number of them, all newspapermen—or even when it took place. Sometime in the spring, I think.

So many things happened that spring.

All that evening the house reverberated to raps and thumps, coming now from one side of the room and now from another. The newspaper persons were impressed, but they were also incredulous. One of them insisted on sitting close by Harry's side, and another—the person from the New Haven paper, I believe—never took his bold black eyes from me. Finally I could bear no more; I announced my intention of retiring.

Even this expedient did not end my martyrdom. With Mr. Phelps's eager acquiescence, the committee announced its intention of following us upstairs and taking up a position in the hallway. I verily believe Mr. Phelps would have consented to them entering our bedroom if they had insisted.

Under the circumstances I felt that it would be more

convenient, as well as more respectable, if I shared Marian's bed that night. Mr. Phelps did not object after I took him aside and explained my reasons—strange gentlemen at all hours upstairs and downstairs. The evil imaginations of Stratford gossips would have them in "my lady's chamber" as well, if we did not take the utmost pains to anticipate and forestall any such charges.

Marian and I spoke little as we prepared for bed. The door was closed, but I, at best, was uncomfortably aware of the presence of strangers only a few feet away. I had not even been allowed to lock the door. This was represented to me as a safety precaution, to enable help to reach us quickly if we were disturbed or frightened. But I knew it for what it was, a demonstration of suspicion. Marian did not complain, though I presume she shared my feelings. Both of us made haste to assume our nightgowns, removing the last part of our garments beneath the concealment of their ample folds. It was an agonizing experience for a modest female; I had never felt so vulnerable. When the plague of clergymen was upon us, I felt sure none of those gentlemen would have burst into my room without knocking first. I did not feel the same confidence in the newspaper persons. Their moral standards, as everyone knows, are not of the highest.

I will say that for the most part they kept their voices down, in deference to our need for rest. Now and then, however, we would hear a loud exclamation and thunderous footsteps running along the passageway. Apparently the knocks and rappings had followed the investigators upstairs.

Having finished her ablutions, Marian knelt by the bed to say her prayers. In her long white gown and frilled nightcap, her thin face hidden in her hands, she looked very young and vulnerable. When I knelt beside her for my own devotions, I was moved to touch her lightly on the head and I would have said a few affectionate words if she had responded in the slightest way. She did not look up. Somewhat chilled, I mumbled through my petition and got into bed. After emptying the wash water into the jar and blowing out the lamp, Marian joined me.

The window was tightly closed against the noxious night airs and the room was uncomfortably warm. The muttering conversations and the footsteps outside kept jarring me out of the sleep I so desperately craved; but eventually I began to drift off. I do not believe I was sound asleep, only dozing, for when I heard the crash it jolted me awake in an instant. The sound was ear-shattering and seemingly at my very side. It was followed by the bursting open of the door.

The four men crowded into the doorway. I believe there were only four of them—at that moment they looked like a multitude— and every eye was fixed on me with a fierce intensity that, even more than the dazzle of the light, made me involuntarily shield my eyes.

Mr. Newson ran to the bed.

"Ladies," he cried. "Are you injured?"

Marian, uttering little whimpering sounds, held out

her hands. Instantly he wrapped them in his and went on, "We heard the most frightful crash against the door. We feared for your safety; that must excuse this intrusion."

"The cause of the crash," said one of the other men. He held up the heavy pitcher of white earthenware that made part of the toilet set. It was not valuable; but it had been in my family for many years and it would be difficult to match a single piece without replacing the entire set. I was chagrined to observe that the handle had been broken off the pitcher.

"And here," the same person continued, "here is the result of the crash—an indentation in the boards of the floor, where the pitcher struck it. It is a miracle the vessel was not broken—it struck with such force as to leave a deep dent."

I looked at Marian, whose hands were still firmly held by Mr. Newson. Eyes downcast, she continued to moan faintly, but I had the impression she was not so disturbed as she pretended.

"Where was the pitcher when you retired?" asked the inquisitor.

He looked accusingly at me; I slid farther down in the bed and pulled the sheet up to my chin. Indignation was beginning to replace my initial feeling of shock. I am sure I hardly need say that I am not accustomed to carrying on conversations with strange men while in bed. My annoyance was increased by the fact that Mr. Phelps made no attempt to remove the intruders, but stared as curiously as they.

"It was not in my bed," I said sarcastically. "You may think women lacking in intelligence, gentlemen, but I assure you I would have observed its presence, even in the dark, had Marian brought it to bed with her."

"Then Miss Phelps was the last to handle it?" the questioner went on, unmoved by my justifiable indignation.

"I put it in the corner, there," Marian said faintly. She turned her face aside.

Mr. Newson bent over her. "Your cheek is very red, Miss Phelps," he said respectfully. "Did the pitcher strike you in passing?"

"Something struck me," Marian whimpered. "I do not know what it was."

"It could not have been the pitcher." This time it was Mr. Phelps who spoke. He had gone to stand in the corner Marian had indicated, and as the others turned toward him he continued triumphantly, "Observe the path the pitcher must have taken. If thrown from here, it would have followed a straight line, striking either the corner of the room or the bureau there. In order to reach the door it must have followed a semicircular path."

"Impossible," one of the men exclaimed.

"But true." Mr. Phelps rubbed his hands together in satisfaction. "The fact has been observed in other cases of this sort. It has also been noted that objects propelled through the air in this mysterious fashion often move with unnatural slowness. That would account for the fact that though the pitcher struck the door with extraordinary force, it did not break." He glanced at me. There was no compassion or affection in his look, only the cold curiosity of a scientist. "What a pity, Mrs. Phelps, that the room was dark. I suppose you saw nothing of interest?"

"I was asleep."

One of the men made a small, wordless sound and nodded significantly. I knew what he was thinking. So did Mr. Newson.

"Let me state at once, and for the record," he said firmly, "that neither of these ladies could have been responsible for the hurling of the pitcher. To hurl it with such force would be impossible for weak female muscles. Besides, we entered the room instantly, did we not, and found both ladies in bed with their hands under the bed-clothes. In order to throw the pitcher they must have got out of bed. They would not have had time to return to it before we came in. What is more, I was holding Miss Phelps's hands firmly."

Marian looked a little foolish when she heard this explanation. Mr. Newson's gesture in holding her hands had had a different motive from the one she had hoped. It struck me that there were several flaws in his argument; what use was it to hold Marian's hands after the object had been thrown and had been heard to strike the door? I saw no reason to mention this. I had not been sound asleep. I would have been aware of Marian getting out of bed if she had done so.

But I remember Mr. Newson very kindly. He never retracted the statement he made that night, and continued to insist that there was no physical explanation for the marvels he had seen; some of the others were not so fair-minded.

Another rather gentlemanly reporter was the person from the *New York Sun*. I recall his name now—it was Beach. I gathered that he had some considerable reputation, for Mr. Phelps was childishly pleased to welcome him.

Though his manners were good enough, I saw at once that he had come prepared to suspect Harry. One would think that incidents such as the one I have just related, among many others, would put my poor boy in the clear. But such are evil minds—no facts impress them when a firm predilection has been established. Oh, I own that persons not acquainted with Harry's true nature might have had cause, in the beginning, to assume he was playing rude tricks on us; boys have been known to do such things. However, Harry would never have kept up with the plan after it became apparent that I was disturbed by it. Besides, as I believe I have made eminently clear, he was not even in the room when some of the things happened.

Mr. Beach had children and grandchildren of his own. He rather pointedly told us several stories about "the young rascals' tricks." I knew then where his suspicions lay; and I was sure of it when he asked, later, if we might not talk with Harry for a while after the boy had gone to his room.

We all went upstairs—except the babies, who were, of

course, already asleep. Harry was in bed reading. He was delighted to see us.

We were talking quietly—I do not recall the subject—when Mr. Beach started and stared at a certain spot on the carpet. I could not see it from where I sat, so I got up and moved to a better position.

The object at which Mr. Beach pointed was only a tin matchbox. But I am sure it was not there before or I would have noticed it, since it was four or five inches long and almost as wide. I keep a tidy house, or try to do so.

As we continued to stare in wonderment at the box it moved, sliding along the carpet toward the bed. Its lid flew open. A dozen or more matches jumped out onto the floor.

Harry was as dumbfounded as the rest of us. Poor boy, he had been so often accused that his first exclamation was "I didn't do it! It wasn't me!"

"That is quite all right, my lad," Mr. Beach said. He spoke soothingly—but at the same time his hand explored the empty air, as if expecting to find a string or thread running between Harry and the matchbox. He found no such thing; and I could not help but feel satisfaction when I saw his expression of chagrin.

Harry was extremely upset. Tossing and turning in his bed, he whimpered, "They want to burn me. That is what the matches were for—to burn me in my bed!"

"Nonsense," Mr. Phelps exclaimed. "Such womanly cowardice does not become you, Henry."

"He has been attacked before," I retorted indignantly.

"Minor things only—no more severe than the rest of us have endured."

"His clothes have been ripped off his body, his things marred and hidden—"

"Please, Mrs. Phelps. You forget we have a guest."

That was always his way, to suggest that I was losing my temper and forgetting my manners. His voice had been as loud and intemperate as mine.

We had turned our eyes and our attention away from Harry as our discussion became heated. A shriek from the boy interrupted us. He had pulled himself up to the very head of the bed and was crouched against the pillows. His trembling hand pointed to a bright yellow tongue of fire quivering on the bedclothes, not far from where his feet had been.

I felt that my senses were about to leave me. Mr. Phelps stood frozen. It was Mr. Beach who sprang forward and extinguished the flame.

"A scrap of newspaper was set alight," he said, holding up the partially charred fragment. "Don't be alarmed, Mrs. Phelps. No damage was done, the sheet is barely scorched."

It was absurd to suggest I should not be alarmed. Any mother would be beside herself after such an experience. Harry, too, was crying and wailing. I was exceedingly wounded by Mr. Phelps's attitude. When I insisted I would spend the night at my boy's bedside he accused me of being hysterical. Was it hysterical to fear a repetition of this dreadful occurrence? If another fire had started while the boy was sound asleep . . .

Mr. Beach came to my rescue by offering to take Harry into his bed that night. So it was arranged, and so far as I know, the rest of the night passed peacefully. When Mr. Beach left us next morning he assured me he would be scrupulously fair in reporting what had occurred, and I must admit he kept his promise.

So, when I come to think about it, the newspaper persons were not as bad as they might have been. The "spiritualist consultants," as they called themselves, were another matter.

One of them was a certain Mr. Sutherland, the editor of Mr. Phelps's favorite publication, *The Spiritualist Philosopher*. He had the impertinence to include us on a kind of psychic tour, whose main attraction was those same Fox sisters whom Mr. Phelps had told me about. As if we were in the same category as those shameless girls, who had made a public display of their tricks and had even taken money for performances!

Is it any wonder that when I first heard the name of Andrew Jackson Davis I took him for another of the vultures? That morning, when Mr. Phelps opened his mail and remarked, "We have attracted widespread interest. Mr. Davis himself proposes to call on us," I said only, "Not another of them?"

"Not another of anything," Mr. Phelps said with a faint smile. "Mr. Davis may reasonably claim to be unique."

"You sound as if you do not approve of him, Papa," Marian said timidly.

"I don't know what to make of him. He calls himself 'The Poughkeepsie Seer,' which rather smacks of charlatanry, and he is only twenty-four years old, quite uneducated, from a respectable but lower-class family. Yet this untutored young man has produced an astonishing book in eight hundred closely printed pages—*The Principles of Nature, Her Divine Revelations, and a Voice to Mankind*. It consists of lectures delivered by Mr. Davis while in a state of trance. Some of the thoughts expressed are quite profound; they suggest an acquaintance with philosophical and scientific subjects far beyond the normal scope of such a man. It is certainly possible that he has been used as a vehicle by spiritual guides of great power and wisdom, as he claims."

At least, I thought to myself, he is not another of those elderly gray-bearded skeptics. Who knows, perhaps a man like that—young, flexible, spiritually gifted—can save us.

The morning of his arrival we were all at the window watching for him. I expected Mr. Phelps would send the carriage to meet his train, but my husband refused, saying the day was fine, the walk from the station short and pleasant. "It won't hurt him," he added. "A spry young fellow like that." This comment smacked a trifle of spite, I thought. Men can sometimes be just as petty as women.

There was no question of recognizing him. As soon as I set eyes on the approaching figure I knew who he was.

Other memories have vanished into the mists of time, but every detail of his looks and his manner of speech remains fresh in my mind. I can even remember what he wore that day—his costume was smart yet gentlemanly—a black coat with a satin collar, brown-and-black-checked trousers, a scarf of green around his neck, and a tan felt bowler. It suited his erect, youthful figure. His long, springy steps required no assistance from the gold-headed stick he held in one hand. The other hand carried a portmanteau, which he swung to and fro with boyish exuberance, as if it weighed nothing. He glanced about with obvious pleasure in the beauty of the day, and a sweet smile curved his lips. He was clean-shaven. His dark hair waved from under the brim of his hat; when he removed the latter, as if to relish the freshness of the soft spring air, the sunlight woke golden highlights in the glossy locks.

I wore my brownish-pink taffeta, with bell-shaped sleeves embroidered at the cuffs, and a collar of fine batiste. It was always one of my favorite gowns.

Soon he was among us, greeting my husband with graceful deference and bowing over my hand. Marian behaved like a moonstruck schoolgirl. She goggled and gaped and was incapable of sensible speech. Mr. Davis favored her with considerable attention, his eyes ever wandering back to her face, but it was obvious that his interest was strictly professional. He was not long in explaining it.

"The moment I entered this house I sensed the presence of spirits," he said solemnly. "And you, Miss Phelps—you feel them too, do you not? You are a clairvoyant of considerable power."

I made an involuntary sound of surprise and protest. At once our visitor turned his full attention upon me, sensing my need for reassurance.

"Don't be alarmed, Mrs. Phelps. There is nothing to fear. These forces are purely benevolent. They come to do you good. They are a mark of favor which few families have merited."

I cannot describe my sensations.

"Some claim they are evil spirits," Mr. Phelps said sharply. "Devils."

"Nonsense, nonsense. But we will discuss the matter at a later time. With your permission, I would like to wander about the house, absorbing its atmosphere and talking casually to all of you. I would also like to examine the notes I understand you have taken. I am particularly interested in the mysterious writings; you have copies of them? Good. And of course I desire to meet young Master Henry."

It was all arranged as he had asked. He spent part of the afternoon sitting quietly in the parlor, his eyes closed, his face uplifted, and the most angelic expression of smiling peace on his face. He roused at once when a clatter of boots on the porch announced the arrival of Harry, who was, for once, prompt in his return from school.

The meeting between them was fraught with significance. Harry's reaction to some of our other visitors had reflected my own feelings of resentment. He had been prepared to greet Mr. Davis with the same outer courtesy and inner contempt he had felt for others, but even his reserve fell instantly before the warmth of Andrew's smile and his companionable clap on the shoulder. (Already I could not help thinking of my friend by that name; it was not long before he gave me permission to use it.)

Andrew then asked Harry to show him around the grounds. They went off together and were gone for some hours, returning with hearty appetites in time for tea.

When the shades of night were falling and we gathered in the library, Andrew was gracious enough to share his thoughts with us. He had requested that Harry make one of the party. Harry was delighted to oblige. He was already devoted to Andrew, and the air of innocent satisfaction with which he assumed his chair and crossed his legs, in imitation of his new idol, was delightful to behold.

"Let me assure you again there is nothing to fear," Andrew began. His smiling glance seemed to linger on me. "The spirits who visit you mean you only good. I know them. You know them too, Miss Phelps, if I am not mistaken."

"I—I cannot say," Marian muttered.

"I know them," Harry cried.

"Now, my boy." Andrew raised a finger in gentle admonition. "Like your sister, you are a natural medium, but you must not be led astray. Let me explain to all of you how the spirits operate. You have all testified that objects have been invisibly moved from one place to another. Not so! The objects were not invisible; the spirits who carried them acted directly upon your minds to render you incapable of realizing the objects were passing before your eyes, or even to realize that your mental attention had been diverted. You, Henry, and your sister have attracted these spirits. You are both exceedingly surcharged with vital magnetism and vital electricity, alternating with one another. When magnetism preponderates in your systems, then nails, keys, books and so on fly toward you. When electricity preponderates, then the articles move away from you. Laughably simple, is it not?"

"Not at all," Mr. Phelps replied. "You said first, if I understand you, that objects were moved by spirit hands."

"Of course. But the direction taken by the objects is determined by the electrical or magnetical condition of Henry and Miss Phelps."

"I understand," I exclaimed.

Mr. Phelps's expression said, "I do not," as plainly as if he had spoken. With a benevolent smile Andrew continued, "Henry is naturally nervous. This condition encourages the accumulation of magnetic forces. Miss Phelps has been made nervous by fear—unnecessary though that fear may be—and is now, I believe, the more powerful clairvoyant of the two."

Harry stirred restlessly, as if he did not much care for

this analysis. His papa looked keenly at him. Then he said, "Mr. Davis, your theory is most interesting. But it does not suggest what we are to do about Henry's—er—magnetism. How can we rid ourselves of these undesired effects?"

"Why, you cannot. They will pass of themselves when the desired end is attained."

"And that end is . . . "

Andrew drew from his pocket a sheet of paper, which I recognized as one of those on which Mr. Phelps had taken copies of the strange writings.

"I recognize this script," he said calmly. "It is like the inscription I read upon a scroll which was presented to my mind some seven years ago. The characters mean, 'You may expect a variety of things from our society.' And this other inscription—on a turnip, was it not?—I interpret as 'Our society desires, through various mediums, to import thoughts.'"

"What society?" Mr. Phelps demanded.

Andrew smiled gently. "Can't you guess?"

"A society of lunatics, I suppose. Only a mind bereft of reason would conceive such bizarre antics."

Andrew was a trifle taken aback by the vehemence, verging on discourtesy, of my husband's tone. Mastering his surprise, he replied, with the same affable patience as before, "You are wide of the mark, Mr. Phelps. I hope to prove it to you before long. In fact, if you will permit me to attempt a demonstration now. . . ."

"Why not?" was the ungracious reply.

Despite his vociferous objections, Harry was dispatched to his bed; and, at Andrew's request, Mr. Phelps put Marian into the state which I now heard described, for the first time, as that of trance. As Andrew explained, Marian was more attuned to her papa's mental vibrations than to his, powerful though they were, and might be expected to respond more readily to his questions. This concession put my husband into a better humor. Taking out his watch, he went through the now-familiar performance, and looked childishly pleased with himself when Marian's face immediately took on the dreamy, peaceful expression I had seen before.

Andrew was proved right. When interrogated, Marian acknowledged the presence of five different spirits. The features of two of them were familiar to her; but when pressed to identify them she fell into a state of confusion.

"Never mind," Andrew whispered. "Don't pursue the matter. Waken her."

"But—" Mr. Phelps began.

"Look at her."

Marian's face retained its look of unearthly calm; but her hands, which had been loosely clasped in her lap, clenched tightly and began to twist and writhe, as if imbued with a life of their own. The contrast between her peaceful look and her frantic hands was unnerving in the extreme.

"We will try again another time," Andrew insisted. "Waken her."

Mr. Phelps obeyed. Marian's hands at once relaxed.

She remembered nothing of what had transpired, but admitted to feeling a little tired. So she too was sent to bed, and then I felt free to ask the question that was preeminent in my mind.

"You told me, Mr. Phelps, that this trance, or whatever it is called, was a therapeutic treatment for Marian's nerves. It seems to be something more. What have you been doing to her?"

A dark flush suffused Mr. Phelps's face. He seemed at a loss for words. Andrew kindly supplied them.

"It is therapeutic, Mrs. Phelps—very much so. In the trance condition the subject's mind is open to influences it would not be aware of in the waking state. Miss Phelps receives the pure and healthful thoughts of her father; they do her good." He glanced at Mr. Phelps and his lips curved in a roguish smile. "Thoughts may come from other minds as well, Mr. Phelps. You know that as well as I do. Don't fight them. Let them in!"

THIRTY

I LEARNED, to my disappointment, that the following day was the last Andrew would spend with us. He had other commitments and other duties. When he heard this Harry begged to be given a holiday from school. I was more than willing; Harry's attachment to Andrew could only be to his advantage. When Andrew added his pleas to ours, Mr. Phelps could not refuse, though he gave in grudgingly. Andrew spent part of the morning with Harry. However, he seemed more interested in Marian, who followed him about the house like a puppy.

When we assembled for tea, Harry was missing. He was usually prompt for meals, if for nothing else, and I began to be alarmed.

"We must search for him," Andrew said seriously. "Without delay."

Harry was not in the house. Andrew led the way into the yard. Some supernatural agency must have guided him, for he went at once to the orchard. And there—I still turn cold when I remember—there we beheld the form of my boy hanging limp and motionless from a limb.

Terror gave me strength. I was the first to reach him, but Andrew was close behind and was quick to reassure me.

"The rope is only under his arms. He is not harmed."

I flung my arms around Harry.

"Mama," he whimpered. "I screamed and screamed; why didn't you come?"

Thanks to Andrew, I was soon calm again. As he pointed out, no harm had been done. I wanted Harry to go straight to bed, but he insisted he felt quite well and proved it by eating a substantial meal. When he finished, I repeated my suggestion, and this time Andrew seconded me.

"I will come up to say good night," he promised.

When Harry had departed, Andrew drew his chair closer to the table. His face was grave. "I must leave you tomorrow; but I will try to come again soon, if my appointments permit. One of the mystic messages still eludes my understanding. I hope to attain insight into its meaning within the next few days. Let me repeat that no danger exists. Remain receptive to the influences that surround you—"

"I mean to do more than that," Mr. Phelps interrupted. "I am sending Henry and Marian away for a few days."

Andrew nodded, as if this plan came as no surprise to him. "And your reasons?"

"You yourself said the children were the cause—the innocent cause—of the disturbances."

"They are. But you wish to test my theory. Good; I have no objection, it is only common sense. Do you, I wonder, have any other reasons?"

Mr. Phelps glanced at me.

"Speak," Andrew urged. "You underestimate your wife, Mr. Phelps. You do her excellent understanding an injustice when you attempt to spare her feelings."

"Very well," Mr. Phelps said, with another doubtful glance at me. "I will speak. I am uneasy about some of the circumstances surrounding Henry's desperate adventure this afternoon. He claims to have cried out. But if he had actually done so the servants must have heard him; they were in the kitchen having their supper and the doors and windows were wide open. Further, I examined the rope by which the boy was suspended and I am forced to conclude that he could have tied himself to the tree. I am not saying he did; I am only saying he could have done."

"You are quite right," Andrew said calmly. "He did."

I remained silent and motionless. Andrew gave me an approving smile. "Mrs. Phelps, permit me once again to commend your excellent understanding. And permit me to explain the mechanism of a process you instinctively comprehend without, perhaps, being fully cognizant of the details.

"You see, my friends, Henry did not know he was tying himself to the tree. A nearby spirit caused him to do so and deluded him into believing he had screamed aloud."

"And you call them beneficent spirits?" Mr. Phelps inquired sarcastically.

"Exactly. From my superior condition I know that Henry was meditating some imprudent act—a swim in the sound, perhaps, which might have caused him to take cold. The spirit intervened to prevent him. This adventure, which appeared so 'desperate,' was just the reverse. You need have no fear for the boy. Send him away if you like; it will not put an end to these marvellous experiences, but it may help you by giving you a period of respite."

So, the following day, I bade farewell to my son and my friend—for such I hope I may call him. In some ways the next week was indeed a period of respite and relative calm. In other ways it was even more trying than the dreadful weeks that had preceded it.

It is hard to explain and harder, perhaps, to believe— but by sheer repetition we had become almost accustomed to uncanny events and eerie sounds. When a teacup flew through the air and smashed into bits against the wall, I would think, "There it is again!" I did not know what "it" was, and I did not like the way "it" acted—but I was used to it. However, when my best scissors were missing from the sewing box, only to be discovered later on the whatnot, I could not be sure whether "it" was playing tricks again, or whether the incident was only one of those cases of absentmindedness that may occur in any household. That was the sort of thing that happened; and so I still do not know for certain whether the absence of the two children was responsible for a cessation of the bizarre happenings. If Andrew's idea was correct—and I felt sure it was—they were innocent vehicles for strange forces beyond their control. They could not help themselves, any more than an electric eel can help discharging itself of an excessive amount of current. (The figure of speech is, of course, Andrew's.)

Though consoling, this theory did not really make me look forward to the return of my children. One may not blame an electric eel for giving one a shock, but one does not enjoy the experience.

The days of Marian and Harry's absence were marked by other events of an equally distressing nature, however.

I had gotten into the habit of remaining in bed late in the morning. For weeks my normal rest had been disturbed by terrifying events, my nerves had been wounded by shock after shock. Not only was I entitled to a period of convalescence; my system actually required it.

Therefore, I was still in bed one morning when I heard a bustle within the house and a disturbance without—a tumult that gradually came nearer and nearer. Rising, I put on my wrapper and went to the window.

The disturbance without resolved into the clopping of horses' hooves, the rattle of wheels, and the bellow of a loud uncouth voice, shouting words that were, as yet, indistinct. From the far end of Elm Street an omnibus approached. Heads protruded from every window. A large glaring yellow sign had been nailed onto the side of the vehicle, and as it drew nearer I was able to read the words painted upon it in staring black letters.

MYSTERIOUS STRATFORD KNOCKINGS, was what it read. It took me a moment or two to realize what it meant. Then a violent flush of shame and anger burned my cheeks.

The person on the box of the omnibus, flourishing a long whip, was the village hackman. His round red face and bulbous nose confirmed the rumors I had heard, that he was habitually intoxicated. As I stared in horror, the omnibus came to a halt immediately in front of the house, and the words the wretch was shouting became audible.

"Here it is, ladies and gentlemen, the house where it all happened! Here you see the door that was thrown open by a skeleton hand and there is the very identical spot from which the scissors grinder ascended into the air, constantly turning of his wheels all the while, until he was lost to view, coming down next day in Waterbury. To your right—"

The fellow continued to shout his outrageous lies,

and his auditors stared with all their might. Every window was filled with gaping faces. Ignorant, evil-minded curiosity wiped every countenance clean of humanity; even the faces of the children looked like masks carved out of some vegetable substance.

I clapped my hands over my ears. As I turned from the window the housemaid came running in.

"Oh, Mrs. Phelps, ma'am, have you heard—"

"Only a deaf person could fail to hear. Call the constable— call Judge Watson—call Mr. Phelps . . . "

"The Reverend said as how he would go out to talk to them, ma'am."

I rushed back to the window in time to hear the front door open. The bellowing ruffian on the box of the omnibus stopped in midsentence and shrank back. From under the shelter of the portico I saw Mr. Phelps appear. He walked slowly toward the gate, where he came to a halt.

He did not speak; he only stood there, arms at his sides. Slowly at first, then in a rush, most of the heads pulled back into the bus. A few of the bolder ones, including one woman with a coarse, painted face, stared back at Mr. Phelps with even more avid interest. Finally, however, his quiet dignity had the desired effect. The hackman's rubicund countenance turned redder, if such a thing were possible. Snatching up his whip, he flicked the poor horses until they broke into a trot and the omnibus rumbled away.

Not until it had disappeared among the trees, and the

sightseers who had followed it on foot had shamefacedly dispersed, did Mr. Phelps turn and walk slowly back to the house.

I suppose he could not have done anything else. A clergyman's dignity does not allow him to shout or call people rude names. I wished he had, though. I would like to have done something—I don't know what—something violent. It would have relieved me to see him do it.

I had difficulty arranging my hair, my hands shook so—not with nervousness but with rage. The comments of the maid who helped me hook up my gown did not improve my temper. I was well aware of the fact that the servants stayed on only because Mr. Phelps paid generous wages and was considered a good master. The girl's broad hints that she was sacrificing her safety and peace of mind by remaining irritated me exceedingly, but I said nothing until she mentioned, of all things, her "reputation."

"What can you possibly mean?" I demanded. "No one has accused you of anything; your so-called reputation has not been damaged in the slightest."

She did not reply. Glancing in the mirror to make sure my hair was tidy, I saw her face reflected. She did not realize I could see her. The sly shifting of her eyes, the faint, meaningless smile, struck me unpleasantly.

"Well?" I demanded, turning to face her. "What is this talk of reputation?"

Her eyes fell. "You haven't been out much lately, ma'am."

"I have not been well."

"Yes, ma'am. Only—you haven't heard what the people are saying."

"I don't care what they are saying. How dare you try to repeat idle gossip. That will do; get on with your work."

She obeyed at once, averting her face as she passed me. I felt rather regretful then; I made a point of never losing my temper with the servants, and I realized that she had probably spoken with good intentions—to warn rather than to gloat.

This interchange made me determined to speak to Mr. Phelps at once. His duties had taken him into town on several occasions. He had said nothing to me of a change in people's attitude, but it was not his way to complain or ask my advice.

When I approached the library I realized that he had visitors. As a rule one could not hear sounds from within a room when the door was closed. On this occasion, however, I heard not one but several voices raised loud enough to reach my ears, even through the thick panels of the door. I thought one of the voices was that of Mr. Phelps, but could not be sure. It was immediately lowered, and I heard nothing more.

Naturally I did not remain in the hall; and it was not until dinnertime that Mr. Phelps and I met.

Though his manner was calm as usual, I saw at once that something had disturbed him. The presence of the servants prevented me from questioning him then; so after the meal I followed him into the library. He glanced up with an appearance of surprise from the book he held.

"Is something wrong, Mrs. Phelps?"

"You ask me that? After the degrading performance I was forced to witness this morning? What do you propose to do about it, Mr. Phelps?"

"There is nothing I can do. The road is a public thoroughfare. I cannot prevent people from using it."

"Indeed. Mr. Davis will be back in a few days; perhaps he can think of something."

Mr. Phelps's face darkened. "I had forgotten he was coming. Most unfortunate. But I suppose I can hardly retract the invitation now."

Such was my surprise at hearing these unkind words in the coldest possible voice that I sank into a chair. "Why, Mr. Phelps! You welcomed Mr. Davis at first, and heaven knows he has already—"

"He has already done me considerable damage." It was so unlike Mr. Phelps to interrupt me, or condemn anyone so flatly, that I gaped at him. He continued, "What has he done, in fact, but spout a lot of nonsense about magnetism, and suggest we send the children away? I had already determined to do that."

"His manner is extraordinarily comforting."

"Do you find it so?" Mr. Phelps laughed sharply. "Then let me tell you, Mrs. Phelps, that this morning I received a delegation of elders from the church who informed me that I must end these—their term was satanic operations."

"But what has Mr. Davis to do with it?" I cried. "As if

he—and we—would not see the horrible business ended, if we could."

"The implication," said Mr. Phelps dryly, "is that I have encouraged these phenomena by my spiritualist researches. Mr. Davis is notorious in those circles, which means that his very name is anathema to narrow-minded sectarians." He was silent for a time, his expression fading from severity to weariness. Finally he said slowly, "I am unjust to Mr. Davis. I am sinning against him in my thoughts. He is, I am sure, completely sincere. You must excuse me, Mrs. Phelps. The threat of a church trial—"

"Oh, no!"

"Alas, yes. It was nothing less than a threat. I am to be subjected to parish discipline if I do not succeed in putting an end to these phenomena."

I burst out weeping. It was not fear of the future that moved me. He had been for some time considering retirement from the ministry. He had the means to do so. But he had hoped to end his days in this peaceful village, enjoying the affection and respect of all who knew him. The stigma, the awful shame of dismissal—and under such circumstances . . . We would never dare show our faces on the streets of Stratford.

He comforted me as a father might have done. Still sobbing, I said fervently, "You do not deserve this. I wish there were something I could do."

But the thing he asked I could not do. No doubt it would have been courageous and dignified to brave the hostile looks of the townspeople—to demonstrate, as Mr.

Phelps said, that we had nothing to be ashamed of. The very idea of it made me ill. It was beyond my powers.

If I had contemplated such a thing, another incident, a day or two later, would have destroyed all my courage.

It happened after we had retired for the night. I was still awake, reading by lamplight, when I heard voices outside—loud, quarrelsome voices. I did not realize the men were intoxicated. Drunken persons do not come to Elm Street. It is a respectable neighborhood.

They shouted terrible things and threw stones. None of the stones struck the house. No doubt their aim was spoiled by drink. But the words hurt worse than the stones would have done.

By the time the constable arrived the men had dispersed, driven off by our servants; and we learned, with the utmost indignation, that since there had been no damage to property the men could not be charged. We could not even identify them. I thought the constable had a strong suspicion as to who they might have been, but he was not at all cooperative. He made it plain that my presence was not desirable, so I was sent ignominiously to bed, like a young child. I lay awake for a long time in a state of nervous indignation.

There was no repetition of the stone-throwing. Perhaps, after all, the constable took steps to warn off would-be attackers. However, every day that week odious curiosity-seekers perambulated the street, stopping to stare openly at the house. Needless to say, I did not go out. Mr. Phelps refused to change his schedule, emerging every morning for his constitutional. He paid no attention to the gapers, but passed through them as if they did not exist.

On the following Monday morning he went to fetch the children. I asked if he thought this was wise. He replied shortly that he had no intention of imposing on his friends any longer. A week had been specified, and a week it would be, no more.

I was heartened by the fact that there were not so many people outside that morning. Overcast skies and threatening weather may have done something to discourage them, but I allowed myself to hope that the worst was over. Even more cheering was the fact that Andrew was due to arrive on the noon train. If only Mr. Phelps would be delayed in returning! It would do me good to have a little private talk with Andrew.

I had a fuss that morning with Sara, who is only six. She said she did not want to go to school. That is not an uncommon complaint from a child on Monday morning; but Sara, who had only started school the preceding fall, seemed to love it. When I questioned her she broke out crying and said the other children had been teasing her. She would not or could not tell me what they had said.

My heart ached for the child, but I knew it would not be good for her character to let her retreat from unpleasantness. My kisses and encouragement did her good; and I promised her the new doll she had been wanting if she did as I asked.

Scarcely had she left the house when she came running back, waving a slip of paper.

"Mama, see what I found on the ground near the gate."

It was a message written in the same strange characters I had seen before on numerous objects. With a thrill of horrified amazement, I saw that the ink was still wet. The child's hand had actually smeared one of the characters.

Sara was completely undone by this mysterious apparition and broke into such howls when I tried to send her off that I gave in and let her return to the nursery.

I sat by the window in the parlor. I fear my embroidery did not progress noticeably. At long last I heard the whistle of the train. Mr. Phelps had not returned. I hoped he had decided to stay for dinner with his friends.

The station is only a short distance from the house—a few minutes' walk for a healthy, young man. It seemed longer than that before I at last beheld the longed-for presence. I had time to fear he would not come at all—that Mr. Phelps had written and told him not to come.

To touch his hand, to behold his smile, was like a soothing medicine. When we were seated, I handed him the paper, pointing out the smudged character.

"It was not yet dry when I took it from the child. You see, Andrew, that Harry could not have done this."

"I know. I have always told you, have I not, that Harry is only the unwitting agent of angelic spirits, who may also act directly." He pondered the message for a time, his handsome face grave yet glowing. Then he closed his eyes. His lashes were very long and dark. "Yes," he whispered. "It comes to me now. A weak, a partial translation only . . .

> *"Fear not, when he returns, fear not, all danger is*
>   *o'er,*
> *We came, we disturbed thy house, but shall do so*
>   *no more.*
> *Believe us not evil, nor good, till we prove*
> *Our speech to humanity—our language of love."*

The words are exact. I copy them from the transcription he sent me later, after he had left us. But no copy can convey the tenderness and beauty of that deep, grave voice.

"Oh, is it true?" I whispered. "They mean you, of course; you are the one whose return means the end of the danger."

"I believe so," Andrew replied humbly. "But you appear unwell— weary and distressed. What has happened in my absence?"

The sad tale poured forth in a spate, in a cleansing flood. I may have wept a little. Before I finished his hand was on my shoulder, gently pressing it.

"How well I know," he said, infinite sadness coloring his voice. "The bigotry of the ignorant—it is a cross all of us must bear who struggle to attain enlightenment."

"You, too?" I asked, wiping my eyes.

"Oh, yes. And," he added tranquilly, "no doubt I

will see more of the same thing, for I do not intend to be moved from my chosen path. But it is more difficult for you—a lady's delicate, sensitive constitution . . . "

"It is; it is. But few men, I daresay, have your strength of character."

He shrugged deprecatingly. "Few men have been blessed as I have been with spiritual aid."

I could have prolonged the conversation forever. Unfortunately, we were soon interrupted by the arrival of Mr. Phelps with Marian and Harry.

My husband greeted our visitor with cold courtesy. Andrew tactfully ignored his changed manner.

"I understand you have had some unpleasant encounters with certain of your fellow citizens on this plane of existence," he remarked.

"Nothing to speak of." Mr. Phelps's look at me was decidedly critical.

Andrew did not miss the look. The hidden emotions of the soul are an open book to him. "Do not blame Mrs. Phelps for confiding in me," he said. "The whole town is talking of your difficulties. I heard perfect strangers discussing the matter on the train as we neared Stratford."

Mr. Phelps winced. Andrew continued sympathetically, "My dear sir, you know as well as I that the blind refuse to see and the deaf to hear. Pay no attention to narrow-mindedness. I bring comfort." From his pocket he took a sheaf of papers. "These," he said, tapping them with his finger, "are the translations of the messages I copied from your notes. Now I understand all, and I felicitate you on being chosen as a communicator of heavenly messages. When you hear—"

Mr. Phelps started to his feet. "I beg your pardon, Mr. Davis. I cannot listen to your translations, as you call them."

"Mr. Phelps!" I exclaimed.

"They will calm you," Andrew urged, holding out the papers.

"No. I appreciate your good intentions. But I have reflected on this and have concluded that in some respects my critics are right. I have been misled. I must decline to continue in that error."

"Oh, Papa," Marian whispered.

Mr. Phelps started. I believe he had actually forgotten she was there. I know I had.

"Come, Marian." Mr. Phelps held out his hand. "This sort of discussion does not do you good. Come to your room."

"Wait," Andrew exclaimed. "A moment, if you please." Slowly he rose from his chair. His head turned; his eyes seemed to follow some invisible object as it crossed the room, from the door to the window. "They are here," he said quietly.

Mr. Phelps made an impatient gesture. "Mr. Davis—"

"One of them stands by your chair, Miss Phelps." In the most natural way possible, Andrew's glance focused on a spot in empty air behind and above Marian's head. She glanced up nervously.

"You feel his presence, do you not, Miss Phelps?" Andrew asked, still watching the unseen presence. Marian swallowed noisily but did not reply. Andrew went on. "Yes, I understand. He wishes me to describe him to you. You know him, but the others are not aware of him. Perhaps they will be convinced by the description of a stranger."

Dropping back into his chair, he pressed his hands to his eyes. His voice dropped to a low, throbbing murmur.

"He is a man of medium height and proportions, wearing a set of Dundreary whiskers. He has a rather long nose; slightly tilted, narrow lips; a broad, benevolent brow. There is a large brown mole on his chin."

I pressed my hands to my breast. A long shudder ran through Marian's body. But the one most affected by the identification was Mr. Phelps. Pale as a sheet, his lips quivering, he stared at Andrew.

"You know him, Mr. Phelps," said the latter. "He says he knew you in life."

Mr. Phelps nodded painfully. "I knew him. Before . . . He was Marian's father. The first husband of Mrs. Phelps."

THIRTY-ONE

E VEN AFTER this impressive demonstration of clairvoyance, Mr. Phelps refused. to listen to Andrew's reading of the messages. He did not forbid me to do so, however.

They brought comfort, as Andrew had promised, as well as awe. To think that we had been chosen by a band of angelic spirits to testify to great truths!

Andrew explained, "The physical and electrical state of Henry and Miss Phelps made it easy for this class of spirits to furnish evidence of their own presence. Thus they showed their desire to cultivate a closer acquaintance with humanity. It is a sort of magnetic telegraph, in short."

"But," I said timidly, "why do they do such peculiar things? Rapping and throwing crockery—"

"Oh, the means of communication may be imperfect at first," Andrew said. My expression must have shown some of the reservations that still troubled me. He leaned forward and took my hands in his. "Dear lady, try to have faith. Some of these manifestations only seem peculiar to you because you do not understand their deeper meaning. Take, for example, the tableaux of figurines composed of clothing. I read in the newspaper a description of one, called the chapel scene . . ."

"There have been others. None so elaborate as the first, but similar in design."

"Yes, quite—figures kneeling in graceful attitudes of prayer, is that not correct? Believe me, these are not meaningless, or—as you may have suspected—mockeries of solemn gatherings. On the contrary! The artificial figures pantomime an impressive lesson: 'Behold, there is no more substance in the mere ceremony of prayer than there is beneath these garments which compose us.'"

I do not understand how anyone can quarrel with the profound wisdom of this interpretation.

With Andrew's permission, I went running off to explain it to Mr. Phelps, who had made a point of absenting himself from all our discussions. I could see he was struck by it; but for reasons I cannot understand he had conceived so strong a prejudice against Andrew that after a moment of reflection he shook his head and pronounced it, "Ingenious but without substance. Typical, I fear, of Mr. Davis's thinking."

"You cannot so easily discount his identification of Rob—of Marian's father."

"I can. He was all over the house on his earlier visit. I believe Marian keeps a portrait of her father in her room."

Against such a closed mind it was impossible to contend.

Andrew assured me that he did not curtail his visit because of any act or word of Mr. Phelps. Of course he is a busy man, much in demand . . . All the same, I know he would have stayed longer if he had not been wounded by Mr. Phelps's coldness.

The morning of his departure was dark and drear. Even nature seemed to weep in slow persistent drops.

His last words to me were a repetition of the blessed verse: "Fear not, all danger is o'er; We disturbed thy house, but shall do so no more."

And he was right—I know he was. If only we had believed him and followed the course he suggested! The grace of his presence, brief as it was, did bring about a cessation of the troubles. It was not his fault that they broke out again later, more virulently than before. This time there was no doubt as to the satanic nature of the visitation, for the tormenting spirits proclaimed their true identity in the very accents of Hell.

THIRTY-TWO

AFTER ANDREW LEFT, I was ill. A form of brain fever, the doctor said; and for once perhaps the old humbug was right. I feel the effects of it yet.

My illness had one unlooked-for effect. It aroused compassion in hearts which had been hardened against me. Foremost among these was a woman I had thought my bitter enemy—Mrs. Reverend Mitchell.

Hers was the first face I saw when I roused at last from a period of pain and evil dreams. I was weak but in possession of my senses; and my chief emotion was astonishment when her face cracked into a stiff but kindly smile.

I learned later that she had sat with me for two days and nights, tireless in her care. We never became friends; we were too unlike. I am not sure she really approved of me. But her sense of integrity was as rigid as her gaunt, upright frame, and she was prompt to make restitution when she felt she had been unjust.

She admitted as much several days later when, my recovery being almost complete, she was preparing to leave me. Being a pastor's wife, she must take the opportunity to preach a little sermon first.

"You must forgive the townspeople, Mrs. Phelps. People are always ready to think the worst of those they envy."

"Envy! I believe I am the most unfortunate of women."

"If you believe that, you know little of the world," Mrs. Mitchell said dryly. "There are children in this town who live on scraps you would not give to your pet dog or cat; young women driven by hunger to expedients I shudder to contemplate."

I turned my head away. I had heard this sort of thing before. Mr. Phelps was always preaching on the subject of counting one's blessings. All very true, no doubt, but unhappiness is not lessened by hearing of the miseries of others.

"You have been ill," Mrs. Mitchell continued. "That is not surprising. But you must make an effort. I will help all I can. I owe that to you. I must admit that, at one time, I entertained certain unjust suspicions."

"What made you change your mind?" I asked curiously.

"I suppose your illness was in some part responsible," said this honest, unattractive woman. "You suffered; clearly you were a victim. My husband always believed that. I rejected his ideas at first, but in time I saw that he was right."

"I am grateful for his support, and for your kindness."

"Should you need me, I will return at once. But I hope the worst is over."

I was sitting up for the first time that day. Mrs. Mitchell had helped me to move to an armchair near the window where I could enjoy the balmy air and the sunshine. Spring had come while I lay on my bed of pain. Fresh green leaves stirred in the breeze and the lawns were gay with flowers. I smiled at Mrs. Mitchell.

"I know it is over. Mr. Davis assured me of that."

Mrs. Mitchell's lined face took on a most curious expression. After a moment she gave herself a little shake and remarked, "Mr. Davis is all very well, I suppose. But your husband is a good man, a wise man. Trust him, and put your faith in God."

I was more inclined to put my faith in Mrs. Mitchell, though of course I did not say so; she would have considered the remark blasphemous. Like all strong-minded people, she prided herself on her ability to judge others. She had decided I was injured and innocent, and she would remain fixed in that opinion unless I did something to change it.

I vowed sincerely that I would not. The good opinion of others is important to me. It is a weakness, I suppose. Mr. Phelps says that we should not mind what other people say if we are sustained by a conviction of good behavior. Men can do that, perhaps. Morally they are our superiors—so the Scriptures assure us. We women wish—nay, we must have—love and warmth and approval.

Mrs. Mitchell did succeed in restoring my social status. There was no question but that she was responsible, for when callers came she was always with them, ruthlessly forcing them to civility and cutting off those delicate, barbed questions at which women excel. Not all the ladies were bullied by her; a sizable contingent remained aloof, but her followers did as she told them, and for the first time in weeks I entertained callers and returned to my work with the Ladies' Circle.

However, I did not receive anyone until I had made some attempt to improve my appearance. I looked terrible—hollow-eyed, pale, almost as gaunt as Mrs. Mitchell. I had lost so much weight that all my gowns hung on me. I kept Marian busy for days taking them in. She is clever with her needle, if with little else.

She was touchingly pleased to see me up and about again, and assured me that the manifestations had indeed subsided. A few panes of broken glass, an occasional rap—nothing more.

I was happy to accept this assurance. I wanted to believe it.

On the surface Harry was his dear self, and far less

nervous than he had been. Yet I was conscious of a distance between us. He was always rushing off on some expedition when I wanted to talk to him.

I mentioned this to Mr. Phelps. He brushed my fears aside. "The boy is growing up, Mrs. Phelps. You would not want him always clinging to his mama's skirts."

I fully expected that Mr. Phelps would suggest I return to share our old room as soon as I was recovered. To be truthful, the idea was repugnant to me. Rest and privacy were absolutely essential to my nerves, and I was prepared to put forth this argument if he raised the subject. There was no need; he did not refer to it. I am convinced I could not have survived without those hours of privacy. It was wonderful to close the door at night and be quite alone, free to dream and read and think my own thoughts. Perhaps Mr. Phelps sensed this.

Or perhaps he had other reasons.

It was sometime in the middle of June, I believe, that Mr. Phelps called me into the library for the purpose of showing me a letter he had written. It was addressed to the editor of the *New Haven Journal*. When I read the opening lines, my heart began to pound.

"Public attention has been called of late to certain strange manifestations which have been denominated 'the mysterious knockings.'"

Flinging the letter on the desk, I cried, "Are you mad? To call attention to this again?"

"Read the ending," Mr. Phelps insisted.

Somewhat sullenly I turned over the pages to the place he indicated, and read: "For some weeks now these annoyances at my house have been subsiding and now, as I hoped, have ceased altogether."

"I felt that for your peace of mind you should be convinced of this," Mr. Phelps said. "You seem so much better—"

"I am perfectly well."

"I am glad to hear it."

I put the letter aside. Next to it, lying open on the desk, was a copy of that hateful periodical *The Spiritual Philosopher.*

"You have not given up your interest in these matters, then," I said.

"There is nothing harmful in them. I refuse to accommodate myself to the demands of ignorant people."

As my eye wandered down the columns of print, a name caught my eye. Involuntarily, my lips shaped the words.

"*The Great Harmonia,* by Andrew Jackson Davis. *A Philosophical Revelation of the Natural, Spiritual, and Celestial Universe.*"

"Yes," said Mr. Phelps coolly. "Mr. Davis is prolific, if nothing else."

"Will you not send away for this volume? The price seems reasonable—only a dollar and a quarter."

"I think not. I am tolerably familiar with Mr. Davis's ideas."

"I have been wondering if we ought to write him, to tell him of the happy ending to our troubles."

"He is on some sort of western tour at present. I am sure he has lost interest in us."

I would have replied, but Mr. Phelps gave me no opportunity. "There is one other matter I meant to mention to you. I have decided Henry should sleep in my room for a while. I have put a little cot in there for his use."

The change of subject was so abrupt I could only stare at him. He took my surprise for calm acceptance; with an approving smile he went on, "Henry is nervous, you know. Your friend, Mr. Davis, said it was his natural state. He sleeps better when there is someone with him."

Heaven forgive me—I did not question or inquire. I was not ready to receive the truth. In my quiet chamber, some distance from the rooms where the others slept, I was able to remain unaware of what was happening.

THIRTY-THREE

ONE DAY in July, Mr. Phelps saw fit to inform me that we were going to have visitors. I have complained of clergymen and newspaper persons, but this was the worst plague of all—Mr. Phelps's relations. They had spoken of coming before; but, like the rodents that desert a doomed vessel, they had been careful to keep their distance while we were enduring our agonizing experiences. Now we had apparently been restored to favor. Dr. and Mrs. Phelps, and Mr. Austin Phelps, proposed to spend a few weeks in Stratford.

Dr. Phelps, my husband's brother, was a stolid, reserved gentleman who spoke very little, perhaps because his wife talked so much he could not get a word in. She was the silliest of old ladies and had never approved of me or my children. But Austin was the one I dreaded. He was Mr. Phelps's son by his first marriage and a man of absolutely terrifying respectability. Mr. Phelps was immensely proud of him, for he had followed his father's profession of theology and was expected to have a distinguished career. I could have wished he was not so courteous to me. The icy correctness of his manner was almost worse than open resentment.

They arrived in the midst of a violent thunderstorm—another of those omens of nature to which I had become increasingly sensitive. Austin had not changed. When his hand touched mine in greeting, it felt like an object carved of stone.

Mrs. Harriet Phelps kept me constantly occupied for the next few days. She was unable to endure her own company—small wonder!—and followed me around the house, talking incessantly. I discovered that she was not the one responsible for keeping the family away while we were suffering; she was fascinated by the subject.

"Did the scissors grinder really ascend into the air?" she asked, round-eyed.

"Of course not. That was complete fabrication."

"But windows were broken; Harry was carried through the air. Oh," she went on, without giving me time to reply, "I was most intrigued by it all. I would like to have visited you then; but you know, Mrs. Phelps—"

"I know. Many of our friends abandoned us at that time."

It was perfectly safe to insult Mrs. Harriet. She never noticed.

"Ah, well," she said complacently. "People are very ignorant of spiritual matters. It is different with me. Oh, I do wish something would happen while I am here!"

They say that God is not the only one who grants wishes.

It was while I was attempting to escape Mrs. Harriet for a brief time that I happened to overhear a conversation between Austin and Mr. Phelps. The gentlemen spent most of their time in the library, talking, as I supposed, of theological matters. How wrong I was in this assumption I was soon to learn.

Never before had I heard Austin raise his voice. The vehemence of his tones attracted my attention as I passed by the room; wonderment kept me motionless long enough to overhear his words.

"I am astonished at your attitude, Father. Surely you encourage matters that are better ignored."

"You have never doubted my word before, Austin," said Mr. Phelps, in tones of mournful reproach.

"I do not doubt it now. I am sure all the things you have described are literally true. I only wonder at your interpretation of them."

"You admitted last night that no one in the house could have been responsible for the sounds you heard."

I could bear it no longer. I flung the door wide.

"What sounds?" I cried. "What has happened? Mr.

Phelps, you assured me the affair was over. You promised me!"

I think Mr. Phelps said something about eavesdroppers, but I was too overwrought to heed his words. The others were apologetic and kind, Austin made me take a chair, and Dr. Phelps stood by me, his hand on my wrist.

"You must tell her the truth, Brother," he said to my husband. "It is far less alarming than the things she might imagine. Mrs. Phelps, your pulse is racing. Calm yourself."

Then they told me what had happened.

At midnight Austin had been awakened by a deep sigh breathed through the keyhole and repeated several times, quite loudly. This was followed by a tremendous hammering outside in the hall. When he got up and struck a light he found dents on the banister, as if it had been beaten with a hammer. Going upstairs, he found the children all asleep and the servants' door locked.

"Locked?" I interrupted.

"I have been taking that precaution for some time," my husband said. "It was necessary to eliminate the servants from suspicion. I have effectively done so."

"But my children are still suspects, I suppose!"

"No one suspects you, Mrs. Phelps," the doctor assured me.

"You heard nothing last night?" Austin asked.

"The medicine I take—for my nerves—contains laudanum. I sleep very soundly . . ." But I could not go on.

Was this why Mr. Phelps had not objected to my having a room of my own? Was my door, like those of the servants, locked after I retired?

Tears overflowed my eyes. Mr. Phelps and Austin exchanged glances. The latter said, "You have had a difficult time, Mrs. Phelps. But you could be of great help to my father if you would."

"What can I do? I swear I am innocent! I am a Christian woman, a member of the church—"

"I believe you." Austin sat down beside me. "I admit I came here with certain suspicions; but what I have seen convinces me that you are wholly innocent of complicity. I hope this statement makes you feel better."

"It does, oh, it does. Thank you."

"Your active participation would be of great assistance to me," my husband said. "I have felt obliged to conceal certain things from you because of your highly nervous state—"

"You lied to me!"

Mr. Phelps's rigid, self-righteous expression did not change. "I have never lied to you. The statement I sent to the newspaper in June was correct. But when the rappings started again—"

"Why did they start?" I demanded. "You did something to bring them on!"

"Not until—" Mr. Phelps checked himself. "This exchange is unworthy of us, Mrs. Phelps. Can you not accept reality better now that we have the support of my family and the sympathy of many of our friends?"

I looked at Austin. He smiled—a warm, encouraging smile such as I had never before seen on his austere face.

"The facts you mention do mean a great deal," I admitted.

"Then let us work together," Mr. Phelps urged. "I believe I am on the way to understanding these matters now."

"I will try, indeed I will. But my nerves will not stand much more."

"They need not endure indefinitely. I give my solemn promise that if we have not put an end to this business by the end of the summer I will send you away for a while— to Philadelphia, perhaps. Would you like that?"

"You need not talk to me as if I were a child, or bribe me with promises." I felt I owed it to my self-respect to say this; but in fact the promise did hearten me. To foresee an end, however distant, makes any trouble easier to endure.

Mr. Phelps frowned slightly but did not reply to my criticism. He was too eager to demand the help he requested.

"Does the name D'Sauvignon mean anything to you?"

The question was so contrary to anything I had expected, I could only stare.

"No," I said finally. "Should it?"

"According to the information I have received, a man of that name was instrumental in cheating you in the settlement of an estate. Wait, I will spell it for you; it may be that my pronunciation has misled you."

When he had done so, enlightenment dawned on me. "You pronounced it wrong; it is a French name. There was a clerk of that name—or one similar to it—in a law firm in Philadelphia. But how did you hear of him?"

My husband appeared a trifle embarrassed. After some hemming and hawing, he explained that one night, when the rappings had been particularly insistent, he had determined to ask questions, as had been done in other cases of the kind. To his surprise he received intelligent answers, spelled out by means of letter of the alphabet— hence his mispronunciation of the name.

The unknown, invisible respondent had informed Mr. Phelps that he was in hell, but had been permitted to tell him (Mr. Phelps) that an injustice had been done me. Mr. Phelps was all agog to check the accuracy of the information, but had been at a loss as to how to begin his investigations without my cooperation.

Needless to say, I was astonished at Mr. Phelps's folly. He had adamantly refused to encourage communication with the benevolent spirits Andrew had recognized. These spirits had now departed—I had Andrew's word for that. Then who—or *what*—had replied to Mr. Phelps's questions? But I knew the answer. It had identified itself as a damned soul.

However, the astonishing accuracy of the information filled me with a sense of wonder that, for the moment, overcame my fears.

"Yes, indeed, there was such a man," I exclaimed. "How amazing."

"Perhaps I should go to Philadelphia, to see what can be done," Mr. Phelps said.

"Perhaps you should. It is not the money," I added seriously. "If a wrong has been committed, we ought to correct it and punish the wrongdoer. He may cheat others."

"Quite right." Mr. Phelps smiled approvingly at me.

"In that case," I said, "I will be quite content."

THIRTY-FOUR

WHILE WE eagerly awaited Mr. Phelps's return, I found great relief in talking with Austin, whose support comforted me a great deal. Of warmth he had very little, I think; but he did me justice and that was all I asked. He even showed me a most peculiar letter, written in pencil, that had been thrown down out of the empty air onto my husband's desk. I remember part of it because it was so very odd.

"Dear Brother," it began—being addressed, of course, to my husband—"The Lord is dealing bountifully with his chosen people. Brother Converse has had the cholera, and Brother Fairchild has grown so fleshy as scarcely to be recognized ... Old Tiers has gone crazy and is shut up in a madhouse ... "

There was a good deal more of this crude gossip, relating events that had purportedly happened to former friends of ours; and the insane epistle was signed with the name of a well-known minister living in Philadelphia!

Austin agreed with me that it was impossible to make sense of any of this. The letter was so absurd that it was impossible to be frightened by it, despite its mysterious origin. Indeed, I found myself smiling over certain sentences.

Mr. Phelps returned the following day. He had found enough evidence to confirm our suspicions, but not enough to justify taking the case to law. This annoyed me. Mr. Phelps, however, was inordinately pleased to have confirmation of his informant's accuracy.

It had been impossible to keep Mrs. Harriet from finding out that the rappings had begun again. She was disgustingly excited, and insisted on being allowed to speak personally to "the spirits." I tried to put her off until Mr. Phelps returned, but I could not keep her quiet on the subject. One afternoon I was entertaining a few ladies, who had called for the purpose of meeting Mrs. Harriet, when the wretched woman began telling my callers about the strange messages.

Mrs. Mitchell was among the visitors. My attempts to change the subject having proved in vain, I glanced apologetically at her—and saw that she was leaning forward in her chair listening as avidly as the others. Her lips were primmed disapprovingly, but her eyes gleamed with interest.

I have often wondered whether strong desire can actually bring about a longed-for result. Though they would have denied it, every one of those respectable, proper ladies yearned for a demonstration of magical powers. Perhaps that is why they had their wish granted.

There was a little distraction at the time, over teacups and hot water; no one actually saw the paper until it came drifting down onto the carpet.

Harriet pounced on it with a little squeak of excitement and read it aloud: "Sir Sambo's compliments, and begs the laddys to accept as a token of his esteem."

Excited exclamations broke out. The grubby sheet of paper was passed from hand to hand.

The ladies stayed late that afternoon. But nothing else happened.

As soon as Mr. Phelps returned Harriet showed him this epistle. He shook his head over it, smiling faintly. "Sir Sambo does not spell very well, does he? Seemingly there are tricksters in the spirit world as well as this one."

"It must mean something," Harriet insisted.

"It means nothing."

"Then I wish he would write me a good letter," Harriet rambled on. "One I could send to some of our relatives—the doubting Thomases, I call them—you know who I mean!"

She repeated this request, half-jokingly, the following afternoon when the family was gathered in the parlor. Only a few minutes afterwards a paper dropped onto the table.

However, it was not addressed to Harriet. It began, "Dear Mary."

Harriet paused. Her eyes were not the only ones that turned questioningly toward Marian, who had retreated to her corner and was bent over her sewing. She had become even quieter that usual the past few weeks, and had taken to dressing in mouse colors—dark gray, drab brown. Hearing the name which might be taken for a variant of her own, she dropped her embroidery and clasped her hands.

"Mama, truly, I did not ask—"

"No one has accused you of anything," I said. "Go on, Harriet. What does Sir Sambo say this time?"

"It is not from Sir Sambo," Harriet said seriously. "The letter goes on to say that the writer is well, and asks me—or Mary—to give his love to Miss Kennedy and to Mrs. and Mr. Davis. Do you suppose that is the same—"

"Never mind," Mr. Phelps said impatiently. "What is the signature, Harriet?"

Harriet's eyes were round with awe. "H. P. Devil," she whispered. "Those are my initials—H. P. Do you think—"

"I think it is a pack of nonsense," Austin said. "It is eminently plain that if these are spirits, they are lying, deceiving spirits."

"I agree," my husband said. He shot me a look of odious triumph. He was thinking of Andrew's insistence that our visitors were angels, from a superior sphere, and that this latest message proved Andrew had been wrong. The fallacy of this argument is so obvious I need not point it out.

The imbecile communications continued, but erratically. We might receive two in one day; then a week would pass with no letter. They were so ridiculous I was unable to take them seriously, and though the raps and thumps continued, with an occasional broken pane of glass to enliven the proceedings, I no longer felt much alarm. Familiarity had bred contempt, as Austin had said. Harry had lost all interest in the matter. He was out all day with his friends, swimming and playing ball, and Mr. Phelps assured me he was sleeping soundly at night.

Our visitors left in August. I would never have supposed I would be so sorry to see Austin go. I had come to rely on his calm, his sober composure, his quiet sympathy.

Things were different after they left. I cannot describe the difference, though I felt it keenly. Perhaps the weather, which was unusually hot and muggy, had something to do with my restless mood. The nights were as stifling as the long hot days, without the slightest breeze; I would have found it impossible to sleep without my medicine. Marian began to show signs of sleeplessness; the rings under her eyes darkened daily.

The summer was drawing to an end. Harry complained of the imminence of school, and I began thinking about Philadelphia. Mr. Phelps had promised we would go if the rappings continued—and they had, though we had come to take them for granted. Indeed, they were partially responsible for my increasing popularity. I was constantly entertaining ladies. It made me laugh to see how they would sit with teacups poised and eyes darting hopefully around the room, awaiting another communication from the air. There were a few—rude, stupid collections of gossip—signed with names like "Sam Slick" and "Beelzebub."

I had another attack of illness about that time—I cannot remember exactly when—the same thing as before, I think, though I believe the heat had a great deal to do with it. Mrs. Mitchell was unable to nurse me. I forget why. Some family obligation . . . It did not signify. I did well enough without her. Indeed, after the indisposition had passed I felt better than I had for a long time. Waking one morning to find the air crisp and the leaves turning bronze, I was filled with a burst of energy. When Marian came in I was turning out all my clothes to see which needed refurbishing and which should be given to the poor.

"Mama, you should not tire yourself," she said in her low, breathless voice. "Sit down and tell me what I can do for you."

She had tried to help with the nursing when I was ill—so Mr. Phelps had told me. I cannot remember that she was ever there, though. She had never been a—how can I put it?—a noticeable person. That summer I had the impression, when I thought about her at all, that she was more or less invisible. Rarely she would materialize, murmur a sentence, and vanish again.

"Nonsense, I feel perfectly well," I said. "You had better sit down; you are quite faded, Marian. Are you ill?"

"No . . . Not entirely healthy, perhaps . . . "

The murmuring, inconclusive sentences were typical. I went on with my business.

"You will be better when we go to Philadelphia," I said. "We might consult Dr. Bishop—he always did you good. The doctor here is no use at all."

"Philadelphia! Are we going there?"

"Why, yes. Mr. Phelps said we would go in the autumn."

"He has said nothing to me."

"There is no reason why he should. But he assured me we would go if these peculiar things kept on happening."

Marian did not reply. I glanced at her. She sat with her hands tightly clasped and her head bowed.

"Well, they are still happening," I said. "Only the other day your papa found another letter while he was alone in the library."

"That was two weeks ago, Mama. Before you were ill."

"What does that matter? We will be going." I held up a gown—my black wool—to the light, looking for traces of moth.

Marian's surprise had raised doubts in my mind, however. I realized that Mr. Phelps had not referred to the subject in recent days and decided I had better speak to him about it. To my chagrin, he equivocated.

"Do you feel it would be wise, Mrs. Phelps? Matters are fairly quiet now; people might start talking."

"Why should they?" I had already thought of this and had prepared my counterargument. "I have kin in Philadelphia and it has been a long time since I visited them."

"Well, perhaps."

"I want to get away from here."

I had not meant to say that. The sentence startled me almost as much as it did Mr. Phelps, who gazed at me with concern.

"Has anything happened that you have not told me about?"

"No . . . But I feel, Mr. Phelps, it is not over. Something is going to happen—something terrible. You jeer at my premonitions—"

"No, Mrs. Phelps, I do not. What would you say to sending Henry away to school?"

A year earlier the suggestion would have roused me to anger and despair. Now I considered it coolly.

"Have you asked Harry what he thinks?"

"Henry's opinions are of little concern to me," Mr. Phelps said. "Children never want to do what is good for them. However, I have talked with him and he is not unwilling." He hesitated for a moment, and then added, in a strange, muted voice, "Marian is the one who seems most distressed at the idea."

"You consulted Marian on this matter and not me?"

"You were ill. It was necessary to take steps if the boy was to be admitted at the beginning of the term."

"I see. But I could not imagine why Marian should mind. She is very fond of Harry, to be sure . . . "

"Marian is far from well." Mr. Phelps looked grave. "I am more concerned about her than I am about Henry."

"She needs a husband and a family of her own."

"Women always regard marriage as a cure for all ills."

"Perhaps. But in Marian's case it is true. She will never meet anyone here; the town is too small."

Mr. Phelps picked up a book. We had had this discussion before; he was bored with it and was indicating as much. So I left the room. I had planted the seed in his mind and could only hope it would bear fruit. It would be good for Marian to spend the winter in Philadelphia—a wider circle of friends, good medical attention. Harry could go to school in the city and we could all be together.

I well remember my cheerful, optimistic mood that afternoon. I should have known. I should have heeded the stab of premonitory terror that had pierced my heart and not allowed it to be buried by hope.

I have tried to remember exactly when it happened. My memory is not good. Too many horrors have bruised it. And that horror, the worst of all, coming after a period of relative peace—just when my poor tired mind hoped a haven had been reached . . .

Well, I cannot remember; but I know it was only a few days after the conversation I have just described. I happened to be alone that afternoon—it was not one of my days for receiving callers—and I was sitting in the parlor sewing on a new frock when I heard a commotion in the hall. I went to the door, to see Mr. Phelps and Marian emerge from the library. He had put both arms around her in an attempt to guide her swaying, staggering steps, but she struggled and pushed at him. Her face was ashen pale, her eyes glazed; she babbled a string of nonsense syllables in a low, hoarse voice.

As I ran to assist my husband, Marian's limbs gave way entirely. She would have sunk to the floor if we had not supported her between us.

With the help of the servants she was taken to her room and placed on the bed. Smelling salts soon restored her; but when I questioned her she only murmured that she felt unwell and wanted to sleep.

I went to Mr. Phelps, who stood near the window.

"What happened?" I asked. "I have never seen her like this."

"I cannot imagine. We were attempting to . . . That is, I was giving Marian a mesmeric treatment—as I have done a hundred times—when she suddenly fell into a kind of fit."

"I have never approved of those treatments of yours. I knew they would do her harm!"

"You never said so," Mr. Phelps protested. His eyes fled from my accusing stare, and turned anxiously toward the bed. He let out a cry of alarm. He pushed roughly by me. I turned. Marian's face was completely concealed by her pillow.

Mr. Phelps pulled it off. Marian's face, far from being pale, had turned bright red.

"How did that happen?" I cried. "Did she do it herself?"

"I don't think so. . . . Good heavens! Now it is the sheet!"

I did not actually see it move; but suddenly it was over her face. Mr. Phelps removed it. Marian's eyes remained closed, her body unmoving, but now her breath came in long, harsh gasps.

"A pin," Mr. Phelps said. "Give me a pin."

I found two—large safety pins. With hands that shook visibly, Mr. Phelps fastened the sheet in place. Marian did not stir.

My agitation was so great that I started to shake her. Mr. Phelps took hold of my hands. I think I struggled with him. I had to do something, but did not know what. When I looked back at Marian, her face was once again concealed beneath her pillow.

I snatched it off and clutched it to my breast, feeling as if I were grasping some animate, animal thing that might move again if I let go.

"Do something," I cried. "She can scarcely breathe! Give her air! Open her collar!"

In fact, she was wearing a gown with a low collar that did not in any way impede her breathing. Nevertheless, Mr. Phelps unfastened the top two buttons and laid the gown back from her throat. The harsh, painful breaths continued. Almost as a gesture of desperation, Mr. Phelps untied the black ribbon she wore around her neck, though it too appeared loose.

Under the ribbon was a narrow piece of tape. Mr. Phelps ripped it off. It had concealed a narrow cord, tied so tightly that it was embedded in the flesh. Marian's breathing was like a series of death rattles, horrible to hear.

"I cannot reach the ends with my fingers," Mr. Phelps exclaimed. "Scissors, knife—something—quickly!"

It seemed to take forever to find them. At last I located a pair of embroidery scissors. Mr. Phelps had great difficulty inserting the point under the cord; his fingers shook so violently I feared he would stab the girl. But at last the cord was severed. Marian's breathing at once grew easier.

Finally she opened her eyes.

"Did I faint?" she asked weakly. "What has happened?"

THIRTY-FIVE

THE TOWN IS whispering again. Or did it ever stop, the buzzing grumble? I hear it constantly now. It follows me even into my own room.

This time I cannot blame the gossips. He brought this on us with his tampering, his unholy curiosity. He has turned my daughter into some kind of monster; he has used my son as a subject for his dreadful experiments.

The first spirits were angels, I am convinced of that. They departed, as they had promised—but the door was left ajar, and Mr. Phelps opened it wide to other Visitors, damned souls from Hell. The proof is in the result—a deliberate attempt on Marian's life. She would have strangled to death if we had not been with her. Nothing like that had happened before. It will not happen again, if I can prevent it.

We leave tomorrow for Philadelphia. Harry is enrolled in school. Marian and I will stay with my aunt. Mr. Phelps will come later, perhaps. That is yet to be decided.

I cannot see beyond the hour of our departure—our escape. I do not believe the demons will follow us; but will they linger here, haunting the empty chambers until we return, or will they go back to the hellish fires from which they came? Will I ever again dare to live in this house of horrible memories?

THIRTY-SIX

A BRIEF SILENCE followed the conclusion of the narrative. Then the lady took a sip of water, and Doyle said heartily, "Well told! You have captured the sufferings of that unhappy lady with sympathetic female understanding. Poor thing! Had she possessed the strength to meet those angelic spirits as they requested—"

Harry Price was rude enough to interrupt. "We know what your interpretation of the case will be, Sir Arthur. Am I to understand that our guest shares it?"

The lady opened her eyes very wide. "Good heavens, no, Mr. Price. Whatever gave you that idea? But since Sir Arthur began the discussion, why not let him finish explaining his viewpoint?"

"Thank you, ma'am," said Doyle. Leaning back in his chair, he fixed Price with a stern stare. "Mrs. Phelps's narrative would naturally reflect the opinions and knowledge of her time. You will, of course, be tempted to poke fun at spiritual consultants like Andrew Jackson Davis—"

"The Poughkeepsie Seer," murmured Houdini.

"Why shouldn't a seer come from—er—Poughkeepsie?" Doyle demanded. "It is no more intrinsically ludicrous than a seer from Birmingham or Berlin. Admittedly Davis's literary works, such as *The Great Harmonia*, are so stupefyingly dull as to be virtually unreadable, but he was a gifted individual, and no fool. He was shrewd enough to realize that the boy Henry could have, and possibly did, play some of the tricks himself, but he also knew that did not explain the mystery. He was right when he told Mrs. Phelps the first visitors were angelic spirits. Unhappily, the Phelps were unable to understand and help them. The modern science of spiritualism was then in its infancy. We know now how to welcome such heavenly visitors."

Price leaned forward, eyes glittering. "So you admit the boy was responsible for certain of the tricks? This was a typical poltergeist case, perpetrated, not by a naughty little girl, but by a naughty little boy. Henry set fire to his own bed and hung himself from the tree—not by the neck, you noticed, but by a rope under his arms. Davis believed he had done that."

"You use the word *poltergeist* as if it were an explanation, Mr. Price," said the lady smoothly. "The name itself is relatively modern, but it is not an explanation, it is only a catchall term for a wide-ranging group of phenomena known from all over the world, and from almost every century of recorded history. We know what poltergeists do, but we do not know what they are. Invading spirits from another world? Ghosts of the blessed dead, or spirits of the damned? Unknown forms of mental energy generated by living persons? Or naughty children playing tricks on their parents?"

"You have summarized the possibilities quite neatly," said Fodor with an approving nod. "But surely even Price will admit that no single naughty little boy or girl could have produced all the phenomena we find in the Phelps case. No, they were all involved, including the Reverend Phelps himself."

"The favorite suspects were Henry and his sister, though," Houdini said. "Almost thirty years later Professor Austin Phelps, the Reverend's son, who was at that time professor of theological sciences at Andover College, admitted that initially he suspected the affair was contrived by his father's young wife and her older children. He went on to say that he soon became convinced they were innocent."

"They were innocent," Fodor said. "In the conscious sense. There was certainly a suggestion, which our amiable visitor has expressed in fictional terms, that Mrs. Phelps came to regret her marriage and missed the lively social life of the city of Philadelphia.

She was a woman of her time, too dependent and conventional to object openly to her husband's tedious habits and lack of sexual—"

"Confound it," Doyle exclaimed, reddening. "I knew you would mention that word sooner or later, Fodor. Have you forgot there is a lady present?"

"It is kind of you to remonstrate, Sir Arthur," the lady said with a smile. "But I am familiar with the word and its implications. I agree with Dr. Fodor that—er—physical incompatibility may have been a factor in this case. Mrs. Phelps's age is never mentioned, I believe, but she is often referred to as 'younger' and 'his second, young wife.' I also agree with Dr. Fodor that she could not have admitted this difficulty to herself or anyone else. It was not proper for a lady of that period to have such feelings, much less confess them."

"So you think the tricks were only that, and that they were played by Mrs. Phelps and her children in collusion?" Houdini asked.

"We know that is what you think, Mr. Houdini."

The American nodded. There was a shade of regret on his face as he went on. "I have never investigated a case that could not be so explained."

"What about the piece of paper that appeared on the Reverend's desk?" Andrew Lang asked. "With the ink still wet?"

"Don't underestimate the kiddies," Houdini replied cynically. "By that time Phelps was in a mood to believe in wonders and portents. He had only to turn his back for a few seconds, or become lost in philosophical musing. All of you know how quickly and quietly a young person can move. Observers always think a series of actions take longer than they really do."

"The most unusual feature of the case is the series of tableaux formed of clothing," Price admitted. "It would have taken hours to arrange them."

"Ha," said the lady, reaching for a cigarette.

Houdini laughed. "I knew we were lacking a female viewpoint in our discussions. All right, ma'am, I confess I share Price's doubts on that incident. How was it done? The house was full of people—the family, the servants, and the investigating clergy—all running in and out and back and forth, and yet the very complex arrangement, clothing stuffed and arranged, one figure actually hanging from the ceiling, was set up while they were there."

The lady blew out a cloud of smoke. "Let us suppose that Marian and Harry were working together. That must have been the case. Only Marian could have tied the cord round her neck; only Harry could have set fire to his bed and hung himself from the tree. The figures and other props for the tableau were prepared in advance—the clothing 'borrowed,' the garments stuffed and made ready. They were then concealed in a wardrobe or under a bed. On that day it would have taken only a few minutes to arrange the figures. Mr. Houdini is absolutely right about that; it takes much less time than one would imagine to carry out a series of actions, especially if they have been practiced in advance. I find one point particularly revealing. Most of the reports suggest that the tableau was found in the parlor. One, and one only, mentions casually that it was 'in Marian's room.' Well, gentlemen, I ask you!"

A servant brought brandy for the gentlemen and another whiskey and soda for the lady, who took it with a nod of thanks.

"So," said Fodor, "you absolve Mrs. Phelps?"

The lady replied with another question. "Do you know what happened to her?"

"Yes," said Fodor. "That is why I suggest—"

"No," Lang said. "What did happen?"

"I quote," said the lady, "from a letter of Mr. Austin Phelps's. He describes his father's wife as being 'in ill health from the first approaches of that malady by which she was subsequently bereft of reason.'" For the first time emotion deepened her sardonic voice. "Do you know what that implies, gentlemen? In those days the mentally ill were locked up for life in dreary institutions, or imprisoned in a room in some far corner of the house where their screams would not disturb the family. It was literally a fate worse than death.

"A stronger woman than Mrs. Phelps appears to have been might have succumbed to the strain and shock of those dreadful months. But was she a victim, or was she the perpetrator of a complex hoax? She might have been driven by her illness to commit acts which do indeed appear to be 'bereft of reason.'"

"Or she might have been driven mad by guilt," Lang murmured. "Nothing more occurred, did it, after she and the children left Stratford on October first, 1850?"

"No. When the family returned in the spring of 1851 the demons did not come with them," said the lady dryly. "Reverend Phelps sent Harry off to school the following year; his name does not appear again in the annals of spiritualism, so Mr. Price would probably say he had gotten what he wanted, and Dr. Fodor would say he had passed through the stressful years of adolescence. Reverend Phelps remained in the house until 1859, presumably without further incident (except, perhaps, for his wife screaming in the attic). He lived to the ripe old age of ninety and died in New York, where he had retired when he left Stratford. His wife is not mentioned again except for that curt, dreadful sentence of Austin's."

"And nothing else happened in the house?" Doyle asked hopefully.

"Not so far as is recorded. It passed from owner to owner and, like so many large mansions, fell victim to changing lifestyle—primarily the fact that low-paid servants were no longer easily available—and eventually was turned into a nursing home." The lady shrugged dismissively. "There were a few rumors of mysterious noises. They can probably be explained as a combination of faulty wiring and active imaginations—for of course the eerie history of the rambling old house had never been forgotten."

"So," said Fodor, "we are at our usual impasse—

Doyle maintaining the spiritualist interpretation, Price and Houdini pinning the blame on the naughty kiddies. What about you, Lang?"

The gentleman shook his head. "I am the merest amateur, as I said. I would not venture to make a decision. It seems to me that trickery cannot account for all the phenomena in this case."

There was a brief silence. Then the lady said winsomely, "I fear I am responsible for the fact that you have not followed your usual procedures this evening, taking each interpretation in turn. My mind does not lend itself to organization of that sort."

"There is really not much more to be said about this case," Price admitted. "Leaving aside Doyle's—er—arbitrary belief in communication with the spirit world, we agree that the children were responsible for the tricks, possibly with Mrs. Phelps's reluctant connivance. I don't believe she was one of the original perpetrators, but I feel certain she covered up the truth to shield the children."

"Ah, but there is something more to be said," remarked their visitor. "You have absolved the person who was ultimately responsible for the entire business. The Reverend Phelps himself."

"Nonsense," Price said rudely. "Are you suggesting he tied a cord round his stepdaughter's neck and set fire to the boy's bed, and that neither of them accused him?"

Fodor laughed. "Your—shall we say lack of imagination?—is leading you astray, Price. I think I see where our visitor is heading. Go on, ma'am."

"The Reverend Phelps was playing with hypnotism," said the lady. "Pathetism, or mesmerism, as it was then called. Have you forgotten the sessions he had with the children—first Harry, then Marian—and with his own wife? He was also a subscriber to journals of speculative philosophy, so-called. In the beginning he was more intrigued than frightened by the phenomena. Confound it, gentlemen, don't you see? It was the Reverend who put the notion into their heads. He didn't mean to, but for an amateur to play with young minds is dangerous in the extreme. In the process, I believe, he affected himself as well. The entire household became victims to a plague of mass hysteria. Once the children got away from him, they recovered. His wife was less fortunate. And he, poor stupid man, never knew what he had done."

She glanced at the grandfather clock in the corner. "Gracious, how late it is! I have enjoyed the evening immensely, gentlemen. Thank you."

Doyle rose. "May I see you home, ma'am?"

"Thank you, Sir Arthur, but my husband will be calling for me. He has no patience with my excursions into fantasy, as he terms it. In fact, he has very little patience of any kind, so I mustn't keep him waiting."

She shook hands all round and then gathered gloves, handbag, and cloak, and allowed Doyle to escort her to the door. After they had left the room, Price gave Houdini a sour look.

"Just like a woman. She has had the last word, and given us no chance for rebuttal."

"Have you anything else to say?" Houdini asked, grinning.

"Well . . ." Price scratched his head.

"Nor have I. Once again we return from that other world with no definite conclusion. But it was an entertaining evening, was it not?"

"Hmmm," said Price.

"One last round, then, my friends," said Houdini. "And a toast to our fair companion, don't you think?"

Fodor proposed it; Doyle returned in time to join in; and then they parted, vanishing one by one into the thickening fog.